Danny Blackgoat, Navajo Prisoner

Tim Tingle

7th Generation
Summertown, Tennessee

7th Generation, an imprint of
Book Publishing Company
PO Box 99, Summertown, TN 38483
888-260-8458
bookpubco.com
nativevoicesbooks.com

ISBN: 978-1-939053-03-9

18 17 16 15 14 13   1 2 3 4 5 6 7 8 9

Printed in the United States

Library of Congress Cataloging-in-Publication Data

Tingle, Tim.
  Danny Blackgoat, Navajo prisoner / Tim Tingle.
    pages cm
  ISBN 978-1-939053-03-9 (pbk.) -- ISBN 978-1-939053-89-3 (e-book)
  [1. Conduct of life--Fiction. 2. Navajo Indians--Fiction. 3. Indians of North America--Texas--Fiction. 4. Prisoners--Fiction. 5. Bullies--Fiction. 6. Navajo Long Walk, 1863-1867--Fiction. 7. Fort Davis National Historic Site (Tex.)--Fiction.] I. Title.
  PZ7.T489Dan 2013
  [Fic]--dc23   2013013183

Book Publishing Company is a member of Green Press Initiative. We chose to print this title on paper with 100% postconsumer recycled content, processed without chlorine, which saved the following natural resources:
• 28 trees
• 877 pounds of solid waste
• 13,097 gallons of water
• 2,415 pounds of greenhouse gases
• 13 million BTU of energy

For more information on Green Press Initiative, visit www.greenpressinitiative.org. Environmental impact estimates were made using the Environmental Defense Fund Paper Calculator. For more information visit www.papercalculator.org.

Contents

To Angelika Douis, who cares for the elders.

Danny Blackgoat, Navajo Prisoner

Tim Tingle

Chapter 1
Soldiers at Sunrise

Canyon de Chelly, New Mexico, 1863

Danny Blackgoat was sixteen years old when he learned a hard truth. Life can change in a moment. Death can ride the blade of a knife or the pop of a gun. You never know when to expect it, but one thing is certain: Death is cold and dark.

Every morning, long before sunrise, Danny Blackgoat led his sheep out the gate of the tiny corral near his home. He held the gate open and tenderly patted his sheep on the back as they squeezed through the opening. His four-legged friends were more like pets than livestock.

"Crowfoot!" he shouted. His favorite sheep rubbed against him as he moved through the gate. "You're getting so big, Crowfoot, soon you won't be able to fit through the gate." Crowfoot was the smallest of the twenty-four sheep in his flock.

As he closed the gate, Danny looked to the sky. The moon was sinking below the mountains and the sun was rising. The sky changed from the dark of night to the blue of dawn. But Danny noticed that this dawn was different. A cloud of dust was rising from the south, turning the sky a dark orange.

"Looks like a storm is blowing up," he said to himself.

He broke into a run, hurrying the sheep before him. Danny led them down a narrow trail at the end of Canyon de Chelly, where they grazed on the tall grasses.

As the sun rose, Danny climbed a steep path to a cave on the canyon wall. He looked down at his family hogan, his home. Built like a dome with six sides, the hogan was made of mud and wood and stones.

Danny turned his gaze to the cornfields and the neighboring hogans. He saw his oldest neighbor, Mr. Begay, carry a wooden bucket of water from the spring to his peach trees.

"He loves those trees," Danny thought.

He smiled as the old man knelt and spoke to the skinny peach trees.

"He speaks as if the trees can hear him."

Mr. Begay lived with his wife in one hogan, while his daughter and her family lived next door to them.

Danny looked to the east, to the rising sun. A small deerskin pouch hung from a leather cord around his neck. Danny took corn pollen from the pouch and sprinkled it on the dawn. Then he said a prayer his grandfather had taught him:

When morning casts its light on the canyon walls
A new house is made,
A house made of dawn.
Before me everything is beautiful.
Behind me everything is beautiful.
Above me everything is beautiful.
Below me everything is beautiful.
Around me everything is beautiful.

Within me everything is beautiful.
Nothing will change.

But change came in a cloud of dust and fire. Danny saw the cloud grow closer and closer. In the full light of day, he saw a hundred soldiers riding across the sands. They were dressed in blue uniforms and held their rifles high.

"American soldiers," he thought. *"What do they want?"*

A soldier pulled his horse to a stop in front of Danny's hogan. He aimed his rifle to the sky and fired.

POW!

Danny's father heard the noise and ran from the hogan. As Danny watched, the soldiers leaped from their horses. They grabbed his father, pinned his arms behind his back, and wrapped a rope around his waist.

"Stay inside!" his father shouted.

But it was too late. Four soldiers entered the hogan. In less than a minute they reappeared, with Danny's mother and sister flung over their shoulders like bags of flour. The soldiers tied his mother and sister too. Danny dashed down the path, pushing the sheep before him.

Soon a new cloud burst into the sky, a red and yellow cloud of flames. Danny Blackgoat's house was on fire! The soldiers had made torches of cloth and branches and had tossed them into the hogan.

Danny gathered the sheep and hurried them to the corral at the rear of the house. He tried ducking and hiding behind the walls of the corral but the soldiers saw him.

"Look! There's an Indian boy! Grab him!" a soldier yelled.

Two strong soldiers held Danny's arms. Another tied his wrists and circled the rope around Danny's waist. They carried Danny to the front of the burning house and threw him to the ground, next to his mother, father, and sister, Jeanne.

"Bring the sheep!" shouted a soldier. "They need to see this, especially that boy."

The soldiers paraded the sheep in front of Danny and his family. One soldier lifted a knife with a sharp blade. He looked to the

Blackgoat family and waved the knife in the morning sun.

"Bring me a sheep!" he shouted.

A soldier dragged a large male sheep before him, grabbed him by the ears, and tilted his head back. The first soldier placed his knife on the sheep's neck and pulled his arm back hard, slicing a deep cut. The sheep kicked and shook as blood poured from his throat.

"Bring that one," the soldier shouted, flicking the blood from the knife blade.

Danny froze in horror. He was pointing to Crowfoot!

Danny twisted and turned, trying to free himself. He kicked one soldier in the shin and elbowed the other in the stomach. He dashed to Crowfoot, wrapped his arms around him, and carried him behind the burning house.

As he was turning the corner he heard a shotgun blast.

POW!

The sound rang in his ears. Danny blinked his eyes and shook his head. His face and arms were covered in blood. A soldier had shot Crowfoot in the head.

The soldier grabbed Crowfoot by the leg. He ripped him from Danny's arms and flung him over his head and into the still fiery remains of the house.

"Kill the others and let's get moving!" shouted the officer in charge. "We have a long day ahead of us."

"What should we do with the family? They'll slow us down," a soldier said.

"Get them to the corral," said the officer. "Make sure they're tied up good. Pick two men to help you watch over them. We'll bring more in the morning. We'll fill up that corral with Indians."

By the next evening, four hundred Navajos crowded together in the tiny corral. They had been captured and herded like animals.

"How long have you been here?" an old man asked Danny.

"Since yesterday morning. I was grazing our sheep. They rode up from the south and burned our home."

"They burned ours, too," the man said, hanging his head. "My mother was too old to walk. I still don't know if she got out of the house."

"Where is your family?" Danny asked.

"It's just me and my wife," he said, nodding to a thin woman with wrinkled skin. Her dark hair was tied in a bun. She turned to Danny with a bright look in her eyes.

"My name is Frances Whitehorse," she said. "And this is my husband, Joe Whitehorse."

"I am Danny Blackgoat. My family is here," he said, pointing to his parents and his sister, Jeanne. They were clumped together under a single heavy blanket, hiding from the dust and noise.

"We can stay together, your family and mine," said Mr. Whitehorse. "Will that be all right?"

"Yes," Danny said. "That's a good idea. Nobody knows what they will do to us. Maybe we can help each other."

Chapter 2
Death on the Walk

An hour before sundown, a wagon appeared at the gate of the corral. Four soldiers leaped from the wagon and one shouted, "Everyone! On your feet! Make a line. Leave the babies behind."

No one moved. No one understood him.

"Looks like we have to show these dumb Indians how to make a line," he said, spitting and shaking his head. "We should just shoot 'em and be done with it."

The soldiers entered the corral and started poking people with their rifle barrels. One soldier lifted an old man to his feet.

"Move!" he shouted. "If you want to eat, get on your feet!"

He pushed the old man to the gate and waved his arms at the others. A long line of Navajo people moved slowly through the gate.

From the rear of the wagon, a cook gave everyone a piece of dried wheat bread. Another dipped a tin cup in a water bucket. Everyone got one piece of bread, which they ate while standing, and drank water from the same cup.

Danny waited in line behind his family. When his turn came, he reached for the cup and drank it in a hurry. The cook tapped Danny on the shoulder. When Danny looked up, the cook handed him a wet rag.

"Wash that blood off, son. Go ahead. Clean yourself up."

The cook had a friendly look on his face. He touched a streak of dried blood on Danny's arm, Crowfoot's blood, and made a scrubbing motion.

Danny nodded. The cook pointed to the ground behind him. Danny sat down and wiped the blood of his favorite sheep from his neck and arms. He turned his face away so no one would see him crying.

The next morning a bugle call sounded before sunrise. The soldiers hurried about, saddling their horses and packing their gear.

One hundred soldiers soon surrounded the tiny corral.

"Move!" an officer shouted.

The Navajo people stood and shuffled through the gate.

"Where are we going?" Danny asked, looking to his father and Mr. Whitehorse.

They did not reply. Danny could tell it was best to stay very quiet. He looked over his shoulder and saw Mr. Begay and his family trailing after everyone.

Walking behind the dancing, anxious ponies, the people coughed and choked on the dusty road. In two hours they topped a small hill and looked down at a green valley. A bubbling creek flowed through the valley.

Danny knew this place. During the long, dry summers, he and his father rode their ponies to the spring. There they filled leather bags with water.

Before leaving the spring, Danny's father always gave him a wool blanket, made by his mother. Then they would ride to the nearest hogan and Danny would present the blanket to the people who lived there.

"Always leave a gift to say *Ahéhé*, thank you, to our friends who live by the water," his father told him. "They are jewelry makers. They'll like the blanket."

The beautiful hogan, once covered with bright silver stars, was gone. Smoking boards poked through the dirt, like broken ribs from an old man's skin.

"I hope they are still alive," Danny whispered.

"They are good Navajo people," his father said.

They soon passed a shallow canyon, an arroyo. A thin stream of water snaked through the arroyo and green cedar trees rose from the rocks. Like embers from a dying fire, burned and smoking hogans lined the banks.

A soldier rode his horse up and down the line of walkers.

"Halt!" he shouted, over and over, holding his hand high. "Halt!" he shouted to the Navajo walkers. "Move to the trees!"

The wagon pulled to a stop. A soldier grabbed two buckets and ran to the stream.

"Line up! Time to eat!" he called out.

No one moved. The Navajos turned their backs to the trees and the burning hogans. Danny stood beside his grandfather.

"No one wants to be here," Danny said.

"You should not want to be here either, grandson. The smell of death is all around us. People died in these hogans. We should move."

Everyone, all of the Navajos, felt the nearness of death. They would never have their noon meal by this arroyo, surrounded by burning hogans. Without a word between them, the four hundred Navajos started walking. Soldiers rode their horses in front of the line to stop them. The Navajos walked around the horses as if they weren't there.

"Halt!" the soldiers shouted. Three soldiers pointed their rifles to the sky and fired.

POW! POW! POW!

Instead of halting, the Navajos walked faster. They passed the lead wagon. A young woman started running. Others followed.

The officer in command called to his men, "Move aside!" He nodded to a young man riding beside him. "You know what to do," he said. "We talked about what to do if they tried to run."

"Yes," the young soldier replied.

He stepped slowly from his horse. He took his rifle from the leather holding pouch and checked to make sure it was loaded.

The Navajos ran faster. Old men and women hurried along. Even Mr. Begay ran, old man Mr. Begay! Dust rose from the road as the crowd of people moved away from death.

But death came.

The young soldier lifted his gun to his shoulder. He took slow and careful aim.

POW!

Mr. Begay fell to the ground. His daughter screamed and knelt over him.

POW!

The daughter fell.

The Navajos came to a halt. They made a wide circle around Mr. Begay and his daughter. Both lay bleeding from wounds to their backs.

"That will stop them," declared the officer. "Good shooting," he said, nodding to the young soldier.

"Thank you, sir," the young man replied. He felt proud.

"What should we do with the bodies?" a soldier asked.

"Leave 'em where they are," said the officer. "They can step around 'em. And no bread today. No water, either. Let's make this a day they will never forget."

Chapter 3
Tumble into Cactus

The second day of the Long Walk, Danny planned his escape. He pulled and tugged on the rope that tied his wrists together. When a soldier rode by, he hung his head and carried his wrists in front of him, like everybody else.

As soon as the soldier was gone, he wrestled with the rope. By the afternoon of the second day, he slipped his wrists from the knot. His hands were free!

"Danny! What are you doing?" his father asked.

"Don't worry," Danny said. "I won't let the soldiers see."

He retied the rope loosely around his wrists, so it looked as if he were still bound. When the waterman arrived with his bucket, Danny held his wrists together.

"I could take the cup in my hands," he thought. *"But I can't let him know."*

Danny tilted his head and opened his mouth. The soldier lifted the cup to his lips and Danny swallowed. The waterman was in a hurry. An older woman drank too slowly and he poured the cup of water on her face.

"No more water for you today!" he hollered.

That night they camped by a small creek. The soldiers filled their canteens. The waterman filled ten buckets with creek water. He and his helper carried the buckets to his wagon.

"Enough water for a week," he said.

That night Danny did a dangerous thing. He waited until everyone was asleep. The moon was low in the sky and only one soldier stood guard over the camp. Danny slipped his wrists free of the rope.

He crawled to the rear of the waterman's wagon and climbed inside. As quiet as a snake, he found a bag of tin cups. He took one cup only, so it would not be missed. He tucked the cup under his shirt.

Before he climbed from the wagon, Danny waited. When he heard nothing, he put first one foot, then the other, to the ground. When he was sure he was alone, Danny ran to the creek. He filled the tin cup with water.

He carried the water to the old woman. She was curled up in a blanket, as tiny as a child.

"Here," he whispered. "I brought you a drink."

The old woman woke up slowly. She batted her eyes and turned her head. She looked at the moon, then turned to look at Danny.

"For me?" she asked.

"Yes, but we must be quiet. The soldiers don't know."

The woman nodded her head. She took the cup in her wrinkled fingers. She closed her eyes and sipped the water. When the cup was empty, she smiled at Danny.

"*Ahéhé*, thank you," she whispered.

"You are welcome," said Danny. As he crawled to his blanket, Danny felt good about himself. For the first time since the soldiers came, he felt good and strong.

"Respect the old people," he thought. He fell asleep remembering the words of his grandmother: *"Respect the old people."*

Day after day the Navajo people walked. And every day Danny watched for his chance to escape.

"Danny," his grandfather said, "you are young and eager to be free. But remember what you have seen already. You saw what happened when Mr. Begay tried to run. The soldiers shot him."

"I'll be careful, Grandfather," Danny said.

"What do you plan to do?"

"Every day the waterman comes in the morning. Then we don't see another soldier for two hours at least," Danny explained.

"If you try to run, they'll see you," his grandfather replied.

"I won't run across the desert," said Danny. "I'll wait till we pass a canyon. When no soldier is watching, I will roll down the canyon wall. I'll hide in a clump of cactus till everyone has passed."

His grandfather gripped Danny's hand. He handed him a stone arrowhead and said, "Keep this with you, Danny. It will protect you."

"*Ahéhé*, thank you," Danny said.

The days were hard for Danny, but nights were even worse. For the evening meal the people sat crossed-legged, leaning against each other for support. A soldier spooned hot bean soup into their hungry mouths, three spoons per person.

As he tasted the soup, Danny's tongue and throat burned. He felt the hot liquid flow to his stomach. He always kept the last spoonful in his mouth for several minutes, rolling it over and over with his tongue until all the flavor was gone.

At night everyone slept close together, still tied at the wrists. The desert ground was covered with crawling insects, some poisonous. Although his hands were free, Danny could not slap away the spiders and insects that crossed his chest and face.

"If the soldiers see me slapping a spider, they'll know my hands are free," he thought.

Every evening the soldiers settled into their tents. Only a handful of guards watched over the Navajos. Danny lay very still while insects crawled over him.

One night a large scorpion, his tail held high, crept slowly across the sleeve of Danny's shirt, from his wrist to his shoulder. When the scorpion came to Danny's collar, it gave a little leap and landed on Danny's neck. Danny held his breath as he watched the scorpion climb across his cheek and onto his nose.

From the tip of Danny's nose, it waved its tail like a signal flag. The scorpion walked slowly across his lips as Danny watched, still not breathing. When the scorpion leaped onto his chest, Danny opened his mouth wide. His belly heaved as he gulped in the cool desert air.

When the scorpion finally stung him on the ribs, Danny Blackgoat quietly laughed with relief.

"Anything," he thought, *"is better than suffocating!"*

The next morning Danny awoke with a stabbing pain from the scorpion sting. Sunrise was still an hour away. He remembered how the scorpion perched atop his nose and waved his tail like a flag.

"My little friend was telling me it is time to escape," Danny told himself. *"Yes, today will be the day!"*

Bread and water were served at daylight. The Navajo people stood as the waterman and two soldiers rode up and down the line.

"Drink!" the soldiers shouted.

If anyone took too long swallowing the water, the soldier tossed his bread to the ground and stomped it in the dirt.

Danny took his cup carefully, keeping the rope around his wrists. The water cooled his dry and swelling lips. As the soldier moved away from him, Danny loosened the rope.

With breakfast over, the marching began. Danny kept a keen eye out for the soldiers. He waited and watched. An hour later the road curved by a shallow canyon. Clumps of bushes grew on the canyon walls.

"Good hiding places," Danny thought. He stood tall and looked as far as he could see, to the front and to the rear of the line.

"No soldiers in sight," he told himself. *"Now's the time!"*

He threw off the rope from his wrists and ducked under it. His heart was pounding. He knew he must act quickly. Leaping away from the line of marchers, he dashed to the canyon.

He rolled down the steep incline. After fifty feet, he tumbled into a clump of cactus. The cactus spines stuck through his shirt and pants. He winced in pain but stayed quiet. He curled into a tiny ball, hidden from the road by thick green cactus pads.

Everyone saw Danny escape. Everyone but the soldiers, that is. The Navajo walkers had watched him for days, freeing himself of his knots. They knew what they must do.

With their heads bowed to the ground, they moved closer together. They closed the gap in the line.

At the bottom of the canyon, Danny lay as still as a stone. He listened to the passing wagon wheels creak and groan above him. He froze when a soldier shouted, fearing that his tracks had been seen. Too scared to move, his heart pounded in his chest.

"I hope the soldiers can't hear my heartbeat," he thought.

Danny lay in the shadows of the cactus for half an hour. He heard nothing—no horses neighing or people talking, no wagons creaking. He sat up and felt the cactus thorns. Hundreds of sharp thorns were stuck into his pants legs and the back of his shirt. He began to pick out the thorns.

Suddenly his eyes caught the movement of a shadow on the ground. At first he thought a buzzard must have spotted him.

"He's flying low to see if I'm dead."

Danny lifted his gaze in time to see a rifle butt coming in his direction. He raised his hands, but the soldier with the rifle was powerful and quick. The rifle butt struck him on the cheek. He fell to the ground, unconscious.

Chapter 4
Burning Saddle

When Danny awoke the next morning, his cheeks were swollen and blue. His eyes wouldn't open. His face was covered in dark dried blood.

Danny felt a gun barrel strike his ribs. He rubbed his eyes and looked up to see a rifle pointed at his chest. He lay on his back surrounded by soldiers.

"That's one fiery-eyed Navajo," the soldier said. He laughed and poked Danny again in the rib cage.

The nickname stuck. From that day forward, Danny Blackgoat was known to the soldiers as Fire Eye.

"We should make an example of him, just like we did to that old man," said a young cavalry officer. "Every Navajo needs to know we'll shoot 'em if they run."

"We can hang him," said another. "It's hard to cause trouble from the end of a rope."

Long minutes of silence passed. Though he couldn't understand a single word, Danny knew his life was in danger. The excitement was over and the soldiers were deciding if he would live or die.

The scorpion sting and cactus needles sent jolts of pain through Danny's body, pain like he never felt before. His face throbbed. But worst of all, Danny Blackgoat felt helpless for the first time in his life.

A strong voice cut the silence: "There is one way to handle a troublemaker that never fails."

The speaker was a captain, with hard blue eyes and a trim white beard.

"Humiliation is worse than death," he went on. "We can chain this Fire Eye boy and drape him over a horse. Tie him like a saddle and parade him in front of the others."

The soldiers nodded in agreement. Danny felt another stab of the rifle barrel to his ribs.

"Hear that, Fire Eye? You're gonna get to ride a horse!"

Two soldiers dragged Danny away from the camp while another brought the horse.

"Remove the saddle!" shouted the captain. "Bring the handcuffs and a rope!"

He ripped Danny's shirt from his back and tied it around his neck. Then Danny was handcuffed and stretched over the horse. A soldier yanked hard on his wrists.

"Oooow!" Danny shouted.

"Give me your rifle," the captain ordered the soldier.

He gripped the rifle by the barrel and slammed the rifle butt hard on Danny's back.

"Not one word out of you, Fire Eye," he whispered in a mean, quiet vice. "You are lucky to be alive."

The soldiers wrapped Danny over the horse like a saddle. They tied his hands to his feet. His shirt waved like a flag for everyone to see. His back faced the sky and the hot rays of the desert sun.

"All right, time to march!" the captain said as he climbed on his horse.

They rode to their places for the day's walk.

"Here," said the captain, "I'll take Fire Eye. We have a visit to make."

He took the reins and turned his horse to the rear of the line.

"You say his family is near the end?" the captain asked.

"Yes, sir, behind the food wagon," a soldier replied, pointing to Danny's family.

"Fine," said the captain. "They need to know their boy is still alive."

He rode in a slow gallop, making sure everyone saw his captive. When he heard a woman cry out, he smiled.

"I think we've found your family, Fire Eye."

Danny knew his mother's voice. He lifted his head and shouted, "I am all right, mother!"

The captain pounded his fist on the back of Danny's head.

"Did I say you could talk?" He yanked the shirt like a noose and lifted Danny's face.

"Go ahead, Fire Eye, let them get a good look at you."

Danny's father wrapped his arms around his mother and sister. He held them close while his grandfather whispered a prayer.

Danny dropped his head and closed his eyes. He felt a deep sorrow for bringing so much grief to his family. The captain jerked the reins and rode to the front of the walkers.

For the remainder of the day, Danny was paraded up and down the line. The soldiers took turns leading his horse. Once in the morning and once more in the afternoon the waterman let him sip from the cup.

"Just enough to keep him alive," said the captain. "Fire Eye is worth more to us alive than dead. But if he does die, we'll parade his body for a few days, then let them walk over it. Same with the bread. Give him just enough to keep him alive."

By noon on the second day, blisters formed on Danny's back. When the blisters popped, flies crawled over the wounds. Soon a buzzard spotted Danny, covered in flies.

Five black birds of death swooped down to get a closer look.

Every day, as the bugle sounded, Danny was led from one end of the line to the other. At the campfire each night, the captain bragged about his plan.

"What did I tell you?" he said. "Since we saddled Fire Eye and let them all get a look, nobody has tried to escape."

"Next time we don't have to wait," said a soldier. "Just find a young Injun and make a saddle out of 'em."

The others laughed.

Danny never knew how many days he had been strapped to the horse. He almost died from thirst. He grew so thin his mother hid her eyes and cried when she saw him. His skin bled from the blisters and his body swelled.

As the Long Walk of the Navajos neared Bosque Redondo and Fort Sumner, Danny was more asleep than awake. Though his body ached and throbbed, his dreams were of the past.

In his dreams, he walked his sheep to the far end of the canyon. He watched them drink the cool spring waters and graze on the grasses. He felt a cool breeze on his cheeks and was glad to be Navajo.

Chapter 5
No Home for Troublemaker

"Take no chance with that boy!" shouted an officer as the Navajo walkers entered the gates of Fort Sumner. "He's a troublemaker! Get the chains."

Two soldiers surrounded Danny. They tied one set of chains to his feet and another set to Danny's wrists. They dragged him from the horse.

Danny was so thin and weak. He lay as limp as a rag, unmoving. For two weeks he had eaten very little, barely a cup of beans in the morning and another at night.

"Bring him to the jail!" shouted the officer.

Danny kept his eyes closed, as he had learned to do. He wanted the soldiers to forget he was a living person.

"It is safer that way," he thought. *"Someday they will leave me alone just long enough. Then I will escape."*

The soldiers dragged Danny to a small building with bars on the windows. The officer banged his fist on the wooden door.

"We have a prisoner for you!" he shouted.

The door opened and a scruffy, gray-haired man in civilian clothes stepped out.

"I don't think so," the old man said, spitting a wad of chewing tobacco at the officer's feet. "You think just because we have all these Indians roaming around the fort that I got to have one living in the same house as me?"

"This ain't no house," said the officer. "It's a jail. This boy is a troublemaker. He belongs in jail."

"It might be just a jail to you, but I live here," the old jailer replied. "And I'm not gonna have no Indian stinking up my house."

"What should I do with him?" asked the officer.

"Do what we should have done with every one of these savages. Take him out in the desert and shoot him. Let the buzzards fight over his bones," he said, stepping inside and slamming the door.

Danny heard every word. He saw the jailer look at him and spit on the ground. He saw the snarl on his face, the hatred in his eyes.

He wanted to drive his elbow into the stomach of the soldier holding him. He wanted to fling the chains against the face of the officer. And when he fell to the ground, he wanted to stomp him.

"Now is not the time," he told himself. *"If I try anything, they will shoot me. They'll drag my bleeding body to my family. I have to stay in control."*

Danny took a deep breath and didn't move a muscle. The jailer opened the door again.

"There's a wagon leaving soon for Fort Davis, over in Texas," he said. "They keep Rebel prisoners there. They'll take him. They've got plenty of guards. And they make 'em work in the fields all day. From what I hear, they bury several prisoners a week. No troublemaker leaves there alive."

"Thanks for tip," said the officer.

"But I still think it'd be less trouble for everybody if you just shot him now," the jailer said. "If you do, drag him outside the fort. I don't want any blood on my doorstep."

Less than an hour later, Danny was tossed in the back of a covered wagon.

"Bring him to Fort Davis," said the officer. "His name is Fire Eye. And I'm warning you, he's nothing but trouble."

"Hey, wait a minute," shouted the wagon driver. "That boy smells awful. If he's riding with me, get him some clean clothes."

The soldiers appeared with a baggy white shirt and worn blue soldier's pants. They dressed him and lifted him into the wagon. Danny rolled to a corner and leaned against the wall, with his knees tucked under him.

"Hey-yo, giddyap!" shouted the driver. The mules leaped forward, the wagon shook, and Danny fell flat on his face. He lay still for a moment and felt the pain flow through him.

"That was dumb," he said to himself. *"I can sit smarter than that."*

He wriggled himself upright and stretched his legs forward. For the next several hours, though the wagon jumped and rattled, Danny felt more alive than he had felt since the soldiers arrived.

He closed his eyes. In his imagination he saw the smoke rising from the cornfields. He heard the cries of his sheep as the soldier cut their throats. He saw the look on his mother's face as the soldiers took him away.

"I will see you again," he said. "Someday."

At noon on the first day, the driver pulled the wagon by the roadside. He dragged Danny to the rear of the wagon and lifted him to his feet.

"Go ahead there, boy, sit down," he said, pointing a rifle at Danny. "Time for lunch."

The driver seemed to like having someone to talk to, even though he knew Danny didn't understand anything he said.

"I'm keeping your leg chains on," he said, "but ain't no need for your hands to be tied. You ain't goin' nowhere."

He loosened Danny's wrist chains and tossed them in the wagon. Danny rubbed his wrists and nodded at the driver. He still couldn't look him in the eyes.

The driver was nice to him, nicer than any white man had ever been. But he was still white, like the soldier who shot Mr. Begay, and Danny didn't trust him.

"I hope you like dried beef," the driver said. "That's all we got for now." He handed Danny two thick slices of dried beef.

Danny took his first bite and almost spit it out. The beef was as hard as tree bark. But a sweet, warm taste soon filled his mouth.

Danny nodded a "thank you" to the driver. He bit down on the beef and ate his first meal ever with a white man.

That night, and every night for the next week, the driver made a campfire. He cooked a small pot of beans in boiling water.

"Just beans; ain't got no meat," he said, handing a bowl to Danny.

The days crawled by as slowly as a sleepy turtle. Danny sang Navajo songs to himself. He thought of his family and prayed for their safety.

Every thought of his home ended the same. He saw his sheep lying on the ground in red puddles of blood.

Chapter 6
A New Navajo Family

One morning at breakfast the driver said, "We're getting close. In only a few hours we'll be at Fort Davis."

Danny couldn't understand, but he knew the driver wanted to tell him something. He pointed down the road. Danny followed his gaze and saw nothing. Over and over the driver pointed down the road.

"Fort Davis!" he shouted. He stood up and waited until Danny returned his look. "Fort Davis," he said again, more quietly.

"Fort Davis," Danny repeated, pointing in the direction they were going. The driver smiled and slapped Danny's shoulder in a friendly way.

"That's right, son. Fort Davis. You're learning to talk."

Danny looked to the ground. A fear crept over him. Soldiers lived at Fort Davis. Soldiers had burned his home and killed his sheep. Soldiers did not like Navajos.

The driver patted Danny on the shoulder. When Danny looked up, he pointed to himself and spoke.

"Rick," he said. "My name is Rick."

"Rick-uh," Danny said. "Rick." He pointed to the driver and repeated his name. "Rick."

Rick said, "Yes," then he waited. He pointed to Danny and shrugged his shoulders.

"Danny Blackgoat," Danny replied. No white man had ever asked him his name. Rick grabbed Danny's shoulder and smiled.

"I am Rick and you are Danny Blackgoat," he said. "They told me to call you Fire Eye, but I knew that wasn't your name. You are Danny Blackgoat. I like that."

An hour later the wagon stopped shaking. Danny knew they were nearing the fort, where the road would be more traveled. He looked out the rear of the wagon. Purple mountains surrounded the fort, mountains topped with shiny white snow.

As they pulled through the gates of the fort, Danny closed the cloth curtains and scooted to a dark corner. He didn't want to see the soldiers and their mean blue uniforms. The wagon came to a halt.

"Hello!" Rick shouted. "I've missed you."

"I've missed you, too," said a woman.

"She must be Rick's wife," thought Danny.

He didn't understand what they said, but he heard the warmth in their voices. He crept to the curtains and opened them just enough to see Rick and his wife. She was Navajo!

"That's why he was nice to me!" Danny thought. *"He is married to a Navajo woman. He* likes *Navajos!"*

Danny closed the curtains and pulled his knees to his chest. He felt confused.

"Why would a Navajo woman marry a bilagaana, *a white man?"* he asked himself.

The biggest surprise was yet to come. Danny peeked through the curtains again. A young woman appeared beside her mother. She seemed shy, even with her parents. She looked to the ground and waited while her mother and father embraced.

When they kissed, she turned her head away. Danny smiled.

"She is so shy," he thought. *"She looks more like her mother too, more Navajo. Her shiny black hair. And how she bats her eyes, those sweet brown eyes. They are like my sister's, only softer."*

"Danny!" Rick shouted. "There's somebody I want you to meet."

Danny pulled the curtains shut and crawled to the back of the wagon.

"I hope they didn't see me watching!"

"Come on out, Danny," Rick said. "I saw you watching us."

Lucky for Danny, he didn't understand a word Rick said. But he still felt caught! Rick opened the curtains and motioned for Danny to climb down.

"Come on, Danny."

"I don't want to meet that girl," Danny lied to himself.

He scrambled from the wagon and his heart fell. A sadness swept over him. Rick and his wife stood before him, but the girl was gone!

"This is Danny Blackgoat, from Canyon de Chelly," Rick said. "The soldiers call him Fire Eye, but his name is Danny Blackgoat."

"*Yá'áhtééh*, greetings," Rick's wife said. "My name is Susan. My mother's clan is Bead People, my father's is Bitter Water. My grandmother's is Many Hogans and my grandfather's is Near the Mountain."

Rick stood watching and listening as Danny Blackgoat and Susan greeted each other in the proper Navajo way.

"My mother's clan is Towering House and my father's is Sage Brush Hill," Danny said, in a quiet and respectful voice. "My grandmother's is Many Goats and my grandfather's is Dear Spring."

"I am glad to meet you," Susan said. Danny nodded.

"And this is our daughter, Jane," Rick said, pointing to the doorway of a building.

Jane took two small steps from the shadows. She never lifted her eyes to look at Danny.

"*Yá'áhtééh*, greetings," she said, then vanished behind her mother's skirt.

"All right, Danny," said Rick. "Back in the wagon." He opened the curtains and Danny climbed inside. Rick laughed and turned to his wife.

"It didn't take those two long to fall in love," he said. She slapped him on the shoulder, but she was laughing too.

"*I wonder where they live?*" Danny thought.

But he never had a chance to ask. Rick and his Navajo wife disappeared inside the building. Soon a soldier flung back the curtains. He was stout and strong, with a dark mustache above his lip and a mean look on his face.

"Get down here, Fire Eye!" he shouted.

Danny climbed from the wagon and hung his head. The soldier saw the chains on his feet. "Good," he said. "I won't have to worry about you running anywhere."

He grabbed Danny's long black hair and pulled. Hard. Danny fell to the ground. He felt every muscle in his body tense up. He flexed his biceps and clenched his fists.

"Don't do it," he told himself. *"Now is not the time. Let him think he has won. Then you will have a chance."*

"I give you a week and we'll be dragging your body to the desert," the soldier said.

He started to walk away, then turned and kicked Danny in the stomach.

"Here," he shouted to a group of soldiers, "give me a hand with this one. Carry him over to the prison barracks. Chain him to a bed. If he gets away, you'll be chained yourself, so do it right!"

Danny spent his first night in a white man's bed surrounded by fifty other prisoners. They were from the Confederate Army, fighting against the United States in the Civil War.

But Danny didn't care about white men fighting other white men. He wanted to be home. While the other prisoners slept, Danny stared through the window at the bright yellow moon, wishing he were home at Canyon de Chelly.

Chapter 7
Mean Mr. Dime

The next morning, Danny was led to a cotton field outside the gates of the fort. Prisoners stood in a small clump of trees, getting ready for the day's work.

Five guards, armed with shotguns, surrounded the prisoners. Seeing the Indian boy, the guards aimed their guns at Danny.

"Just give me a reason," said a guard, "and I'll blow you to kingdom come."

Danny didn't understand the words, but he understood the message. The prisoners laughed.

"What's your name, boy?" a prisoner asked.

He was short and stout. His arms hung to below his knees and rippled with muscles. Danny kept his eyes to the ground.

"I'm asking you a question, boy!" the prisoner said.

"He's just a dumb Indian," said another prisoner. "He talks Indian talk."

"I ain't working with no Indian," said the stout man. He lifted Danny's chin and leaned in close to his face.

"See if you understand this, boy," he said.

He swallowed and rolled a wad of spit in his mouth. He leaned back his head and spit in Danny's face. Danny covered his face with his hands and the prisoner shoved him hard in the chest. Danny fell to the ground.

"Understand *that*?" the prisoner shouted. "We don't like you!"

The others laughed and the prisoner turned away. But the day's battle had just begun.

Danny leaped to his feet. While the guards and prisoners watched, Danny snuck up behind the bullying man. He tapped him on the shoulder, softly. When the stout man turned, he showed surprise on his face.

"Well," he said with a sneer.

That was all he had time to say. Danny bent his knees, crouching low and clenching his fist. He leaped up and smashed the man in the face, knocking him to the ground.

"You're gonna be sorry you did that, boy," he said, wiping blood from his lip and scrambling to his feet. He grabbed Danny by the collar.

"No more!" a voice shouted.

A powerful arm fell like a tree trunk between Danny and the bully. The powerful arm belonged to a prisoner, an older man with a huge chest and round belly. He had a gray beard and white hair.

"Give him a chance," said the man. "Let's see if this Indian boy can work."

"Jim Davis, you saw what this boy did," said the bully. "I'm gonna kill him for it."

"No, Mr. Dime. You're not killing anybody this morning," said Davis. "You're going to work, same as the rest of us."

"You better listen to him," said a soldier, nudging Mr. Dime with his rifle. "No more fighting today. It's time to work."

Mr. Dime shook his fist and gave Danny a long, mean look.

"This ain't over yet," he said, and turned to the cotton fields.

"Davis!" said the soldier. "Help this boy get started. See what he can do."

"What's his name?" asked Davis.

"The officer called him Fire Eye. He said he was a troublemaker. Didn't take him long."

"Well," said Davis, "the boy didn't start it. But he sure picked the wrong man to fight."

The soldiers moved to the fields to guard the prisoners. Davis turned to Danny, who was leaning against a tree and staring at the ground.

"Fire Eye!" he said. Danny didn't move. "That's not your name, is it?"

Danny said nothing. Davis picked up a hoe and took Danny by the arm.

"Let's get started, son. I'll figure out what to call you later. For now, you're Fire Eye."

He led Danny as far away from Mr. Dime and his friends as possible, to the far side of the cotton field. He finally halted in a patch of thick weeds at the base of a hill.

"Here," he said, "watch what I do."

Davis grabbed the hoe by the handle. He cut a new row into the hard, dry ground and then yanked out the weeds by the roots. After five minutes of hoeing, he tossed the hoe at Danny's feet.

"Your turn," he said. "Give it a try."

Danny picked up the hoe and continued cutting the row Jim Davis had started. He didn't look up. He went about the work as if he had been doing it every day for weeks. He pulled the weeds, shook off the dirt from the roots, and tossed them in a pile.

Davis wiped the sweat from his brow and smiled.

"I believe you know how to work, son," he whispered to himself.

Davis looked across the fields at the other prisoners. They were leaning on their hoes and talking. If a soldier hollered, they returned to work, but as soon as the soldier turned away, they stopped.

"We could all learn something from this young man," Davis said.

Thirty minutes later, Davis touched Danny on the shoulder.

"Fire Eye, I think you know what you're doing. I'll get another hoe and start at the far end. Meet you in the middle!"

Danny said nothing, but he saw the smile on Jim Davis's face. He nodded and went back to work. He watched as Davis began hoeing at the other end of the row.

"We will meet in the middle," he thought. *"I like this man. I acted like a fool and he saved my life."*

Chapter 8
Danny Saves a Friend

"Lunchtime!" a guard shouted. The sun shone high overhead. Danny looked to Jim Davis, who leaned on his hoe only twenty feet away.

"We done good this morning," Davis said. "You're a good worker."

The prisoners laid down their tools and made their way to the shade of the trees. They sat in groups, on logs and on the ground. A cook served bowls of beans from the back of a wagon.

Davis sat beside Danny, protecting him from Mr. Dime.

"You can't watch him forever," Dime said. "I'm gonna kill that boy. You wait and see."

"Your killing days are over, Dime," said a guard. "I'm tired of burying anybody you pick a fight with. No more, you hear me?"

When the day's work was finished, they returned to the prison barracks. As they neared the building, a guard yanked Danny's arm and dragged him through the door. He shoved him on his bed, face down, and chained his hands and feet to the bed.

"Any more trouble out of you and I will kill you myself," he said and turned to go.

After a week of hard work, Danny earned the respect of the guards, and some of the prisoners. He was no longer chained to his bed. But many times a day he felt the mean glare of Mr. Dime, waiting for his time to get even.

One morning, as the prisoners finished their coffee by the campfire, Davis stood up.

"Time we get to work," he said.

The prisoners tossed back their final swallow of coffee. But Davis didn't take another step. Instead, he grabbed his chest with both hands.

As Danny watched, Davis slumped over and began breathing hard. His face turned white and his eyes rolled back in his head. The men laughed.

"Did somebody shoot you, Jim?" a prisoner asked.

Davis didn't reply.

The prisoners laughed harder, thinking Davis was joking. Davis rocked back and forth. His arms fell to his sides.

"Somebody call a doctor!" joked the prisoner.

The men howled with laughter. But Danny knew that Jim Davis was not making a joke. He was dying in front of them and the men were laughing.

Danny had watched his grandfather save Mr. Begay's life seven years ago. Mr. Begay had grabbed his chest and fallen to the ground. His grandfather beat him on the chest with both fists. When Mr. Begay's face turned white, he blew air into his mouth.

Danny closed his eyes and remembered every detail. He was only nine years old, but he never forgot the day his grandfather saved Mr. Begay's life.

When Davis fell backwards and landed on the fire, the men grew silent.

"He is hurt," the prisoner said.

Danny knew what to do. He leaped to his friend. He rolled him out of the fire and on his back. While the soldiers and prisoners watched, Danny took a deep breath. He opened Davis's mouth and blew air into it. Then he doubled up his fist and pounded hard on his chest.

For several long minutes, as the others stood frozen, Danny Blackgoat pounded his friend's chest and blew air into his lungs. Finally, Davis opened his eyes.

"Wha . . . wha . . . what did?" Davis stammered, unable to speak.

More than ever, Danny wished he had the words to say. He patted Davis on the chest and looked into his eyes. Davis closed his eyes again, but Danny felt his chest move up and down.

"He is breathing," he thought. *"He will live."*

"Let's get him to the doctor," a soldier said.

As three strong prisoners carried him away, Davis moved his lips, searching for the words.

He lifted his head, looking for Danny. When he spotted him, he took a deep breath.

"You saved my life, Fire Eye," Jim Davis said.

Danny nodded and lifted his palm to his friend.

"Back to work!" a guard shouted.

Danny took his hoe and hurried to the far side of the cotton row. The prisoners moved quietly back to the fields. No one spoke. Everyone walked with their eyes to the ground. Jim Davis was the only man that every prisoner respected and every prisoner liked. He was their friend.

Danny worked with a madness. He raised his hoe high and flung his whole body into the swing, burying the blade deep into the cracked brown dirt.

"Why did this happen to Jim Davis?" he asked himself.

Over and over he swung his hoe, until it slipped from his grip and sailed over his head. Danny watched the hoe and his eyes grew big. The hoe was flying toward a group of prisoners and Mr. Dime was one of them! He was on his knees, planting cottonseed.

The wooden hoe handle struck Mr. Dime in the back of the neck. He fell forward, but not for long. He jumped to his feet and picked up Danny's hoe.

"It's that Indian boy's hoe!" shouted a prisoner.

Mr. Dime slowly turned to face the boy. Danny stood and waited. When Mr. Dime started walking in his direction, Danny wanted to run. He knew what Mr. Dime would do to him, with no Jim Davis to stand in his way.

But today was not a day for running. Jim Davis had almost died. This was a day for facing his enemy. Mr. Dime expected him to run.

"Circle him, so he can't get away!" he shouted.

Now Danny Blackgoat ran, but not as Mr. Dime expected. He ran as fast as he could, straight at the bullying man. When Danny grew close, Mr. Dime crouched into a fighting stance and lifted his fists. Danny didn't slow down. He didn't circle his enemy like a boxer would do.

No, he ran faster still. When he was five feet from Mr. Dime, he planted his left foot hard and jumped. He hit Mr. Dime in the right kneecap with both feet.

"Ooooow!" Mr. Dime cried out.

He rolled on his belly and grabbed his knee with both hands. Danny leaped on his back and grabbed his hair, just like Mr. Dime had done to him that first day in the fields. He slammed his head in the dirt, three, four, five times.

But Mr. Dime was strong. He was also proud. He ignored the pain in his knee and reached behind himself. He took Danny's wrists and flung the boy over his head and to the ground. Then he rose and walked toward Danny.

He leaned over and picked up Danny's hoe. Without stopping, he whipped the hoe handle and landed a hard blow to Danny's back. Danny felt a flash of pain through his whole body. Mr. Dime smiled and flipped the hoe from one hand to the next. He now held it so the next blow would sink the blade into the troublemaking Indian boy.

"One blow and you're dead, Fire Eye," he said with a sneer on his face. "Are you ready for that?"

Danny said nothing. He met Mr. Dime's strong gaze with one of his own.

"Maybe Jim Davis and I will die on the same day," Danny thought. *"Maybe it is meant to be."*

"Let's put it to a vote," Mr. Dime said. "So, who wants to bury this boy today, right here in the cotton field?"

He turned and expected his fellow prisoners to cheer him on. Instead, no one said a word.

For the first time in Mr. Dime's life, the other prisoners were standing up to him. They looked at Danny Blackgoat and saw a brave young man, a young man who had done something they had never had the courage to do themselves. This Indian boy had thrown himself at the meanest bully they had ever known, a man known for killing a dozen men.

Mr. Dime asked again, "Who wants to help me kill this animal?"

One by one the men turned away. They picked up their hoes and walked back to work. If Mr. Dime wanted to kill the Indian, he would have to do it on his own.

Mr. Dime cursed the other prisoners. "You are no better than he is, you bunch of cowards!" he called to them as they moved away.

When he turned to Danny, the boy stood his ground. Mr. Dime struck him in the face with the handle. Danny tried to block the blow with his wrist, but Mr. Dime was powerful. In a few minutes he stood over Danny, kicking him again and again.

"That's enough!" shouted the guard.

POW!

He fired his shotgun into the air to make his point. Mr. Dime picked up his basket of cottonseeds and walked away, leaving Danny Blackgoat lying in a pool of dark blood. Two prisoners carried him to his cot in the barracks. Danny moaned in agony. Whichever way he rolled, a new pain shot though him.

"Lie still for a moment," a man's voice commanded.

Danny looked up to see a soldier he had never seen before.

"I'm a doctor," the man said. "I'm here to help you."

"He's an Indian," said a prisoner. "He don't know how to talk."

The doctor nodded and turned to Danny. He moved a finger to his lips, telling Danny to be quiet. Then he held his palms in front of him and moved them up and down slowly, telling Danny to stay still. Danny relaxed.

The doctor picked up Danny's arms, one at a time. He lifted his legs, too.

After ten minutes, he stood and said, "Well, he doesn't have any broken bones. He's lucky. He wouldn't be the first man Mr. Dime killed."

Chapter 9
Mr. Dime and the Rattlesnake

Danny stayed in bed for the next two days. On the morning of the third day, he returned to the cotton field. While the other prisoners drank their coffee, he lingered on the edge of the campfire. He wanted to avoid the glaring eyes of Mr. Dime.

"Look who's come to work today," Mr. Dime said. "You ready for a real whipping, boy?"

"There won't be any more whipping, Dime. I've got my eyes on you," a soldier said. "This boy came back to work and that's what he's gonna do, same as you. Now, let's get started!"

The guard handed him a basket of seeds, but Danny shook his head.

"It's your life," said the soldier.

He lifted Danny's hoe from the back of the supply wagon and tossed it at his feet.

"Just remember," he warned, "it's not a weapon."

Mr. Dime stared hard at Danny. On his way to the field he stuck his hoe handle in front of Danny, trying to trip him.

Danny was ready. He turned around and walked away, to the far side of the cotton rows.

"I know his plan," Danny thought. *"He will leave me alone mostly. But he will never forget what I did, how I fought him back. One day, when everybody has forgotten about him wanting to kill me, Mr. Dime will come at me. I know he will. He'll wait till dark and try to kill me."*

A week later, an hour before dawn, Danny felt a strong hand on his shoulder. He was asleep in the barracks. When he opened his eyes, there stood Jim Davis. He sat up, surprised to see his friend.

"Didn't think you'd ever see me again, did you?" Davis asked. "I snuck out. I'm not supposed to be walking yet, but I had to come see you. I can't stay long."

Davis sat on the edge of the bed.

"I don't know how to talk so you'll understand me. But I'm gonna try anyway."

Davis gripped Danny on the shoulder and looked him in the eyes.

"Thank you, Fire Eye," Davis said. "You saved my life. I will never forget that."

He pounded his chest with his fists, smiling. Then he took a deep breath till his cheeks swelled, still pounding on his chest. Finally, Danny smiled, too.

"Good," said Davis. "You understand me. Thank you," he repeated, and Danny nodded.

"I wanted to tell you," Davis continued, "I'm not working in the fields anymore."

He pointed to the fields and made a hoeing motion with his arms.

"No field work for Jim Davis," he said, shaking his head.

"No?" Danny asked.

"Well, you are understanding," said Davis. "I am the carpenter now."

Davis pointed in the other direction.

"Car-pen-ter," he said slowly.

"Car-pen-ter," Danny echoed.

"Yes," said Davis. "I build things. Like coffins, when somebody dies."

Danny tilted his head in a questioning way.

"You don't understand yet," said Davis, "but you will. I'll make sure you do. But I better go before they catch me."

He waved good-bye and slipped out the door.

"*Ahéhé*," Danny whispered to himself. He opened his deerskin pouch and tossed corn pollen to the morning sun.

The night after Jim Davis's visit, Danny had the worst dream since his arrival at Fort Davis.

"Your dreams are important," Danny's grandfather always told him. "They carry warnings. No one should ignore their dreams."

Danny dreamed he was digging tall weeds in the cotton field. He heard something in the grass. When he parted the weeds to take a look, a giant lizard rose far over Danny's head.

The lizard opened its mouth and flashed two rows of shiny, sharp teeth. He pulled back his head and sank his teeth into Danny's chest. Danny called out, but nobody came to help him. The lizard lifted him from the ground and tossed him across the field. Danny fell at the feet of Mr. Dime.

"I see you've come for your punishment," Dime said. And just as he was raising his hoe to strike, Danny woke up.

He was sweating and breathing hard. He glanced around the barracks. The other prisoners were snoring as usual.

"I guess they didn't hear me," he whispered to himself.

But Danny couldn't get back to sleep. He sat on the edge of his bed and remembered the words of his grandfather: "No one should ignore their dreams."

"I should be very careful today," he thought.

Danny had coffee and breakfast with the other prisoners that morning. He kept his eyes to the ground, as usual. But he knew exactly where Mr. Dime sat. And when the prisoners rose to go, he grabbed his hoe and walked quickly to the field before Mr. Dime finished his coffee.

Danny's dream came true in less than an hour. He saw the dry weeds move and sway before he heard anything. When he did hear the sound, it was stronger than he expected.

WHIRRRRR.

Danny knew this sound. Many mornings while his sheep grazed in the canyon, he had heard this sound.

"Rattlesnake," Danny thought. *"That's the lizard of my dreams!"*

He turned to the other prisoners, wanting to warn them. But he didn't know what to say. When he looked to the weeds, the snake lifted himself high and waved his head back and forth. He opened his mouth and Danny saw two large fangs.

As the snake struck, Danny raised his hoe and caught the blow. He dropped the hoe and ran across the field to the guards.

"Hey, hey!" he shouted. "Hey, hey!"

"What is it?" asked a guard.

Danny lifted his arm and moved it back and forth in the motion of a snake. Then he opened his fingers wide and made a striking motion, flinging his arm forward.

"A rattlesnake," said a guard. "He's telling us there's a snake in the fields."

Danny pointed to the spot where his hoe lay. The guard readied the firing pin on his shotgun and moved quickly across the field.

"There it is!" he shouted.

He raised his rifle and fired, but the shot missed.

"He got away," he said, kicking the dirt.

"All right, men," said an officer, turning to the prisoners. "The excitement is over. Nobody's hurt, so get back to work. Be careful where you step. If there's one rattlesnake, there are others."

At the noon meal, Danny saw Mr. Dime talking quietly to a group of prisoners. Those prisoners spoke to others, but never when the guards were around.

"He must be planning something," Danny thought.

Danny was right. But what Mr. Dime was planning was so dark and evil, Danny would never guess it.

Just before quitting time, Danny saw a flurry of movement from a group of prisoners. They pointed to the ground and backed away.

"They've spotted a snake," Danny thought.

"What is it?" shouted a guard.

"Nothing," said Mr. Dime. "Just a prairie dog. These men are scared of their own shadows today!"

But the men did not return to the cotton row. They moved to another row, all but Mr. Dime. When the guard looked away, Mr. Dime emptied his bag of cotton. He slapped the ground hard with his hoe, then tossed the hoe aside. Holding his bag in front of him, he jumped into the bushes.

"He's trying to catch the snake," Danny thought.

Mr. Dime disappeared between the cotton rows.

On the far side of the cotton field a prisoner shouted, "Here's another snake!"

The guards turned their attention to this new disturbance.

"Leave him alone!" shouted a guard. "It's time for supper. Come on!"

"There was no second rattlesnake," Danny thought. *"They were giving Mr. Dime time to catch the snake without the guards knowing it."*

On the way to the supper wagon a guard said, "We'll have the young soldiers look for snakes after supper. They'll have the fields safe by morning."

Mr. Dime stayed behind the other prisoners. Danny watched him hide his cotton bag in the bushes near the campfire. He dug a hole and buried the bag, placing a heavy stone on top of it.

Danny also saw the bag move. The rattlesnake whipped its body back and forth as it was buried.

"What does he plan to do with the snake?"

Chapter 10
Death of Fire Eye

That night, after everyone was sound asleep and snoring, Danny crawled from his bed. He crept slowly from one creaking board to another and slipped outside. Clouds covered the moon.

Danny stayed close to the buildings and away from any windows. He moved through the shadows until he came to the door of the carpenter shop. The door was unlocked, so he entered. Closing the door behind himself, Danny froze.

"What if Jim Davis is not alone?" he thought. *"What if someone else lives here too?"*

"Who is it?" a voice boomed.

Danny leaned against the door without moving.

"Fire Eye?" Jim Davis asked. "Is that you?"

Danny said nothing. He moved to the bedside of his friend. Davis laughed and patted the bed.

"Here," he said, "have a seat while I get dressed."

Danny hung his head and waited, embarrassed at what he had done.

"I'm glad you came," Davis said. "Let's go outside. No need to be afraid."

He opened the door and Danny followed. Davis sat on the porch step and Danny sat beside him. The two sat without speaking for a long time. Finally, Davis moved his hand to Danny. He lifted his chin until Danny looked him in the eyes.

"Son," Davis said, "you won't know what I'm saying. Not yet. But I've been thinking about this for a while. You are smart. That's why you are trouble for the soldiers."

Danny stared at his friend.

"You need to learn how to talk, son. Two languages. And I know your name is not Fire Eye. I don't want to call you that anymore."

Davis pointed to his chest.

"My name is Jim Davis," he said. He tapped himself on the chest. "Jim Davis."

Danny nodded.

"Say it, son. Jim Davis."

"Gee-um Day-vis," Danny said, slowly and carefully.

"That's it, son! Say it again!" Davis stood and patted his chest with his palm.

"Jim Day-vis," Danny said.

"Yes! Again! Say it again!" Davis shouted.

Danny smiled and pointed to his friend. "Jim Davis," he said.

Davis threw his head back and laughed. He pulled Danny to his chest and gave him a powerful hug.

"Jim Davis," Danny said, his voice muffled.

"Now," Davis said. "I want to know *your* name. I know it's not Fire Eye. I want to know your *real* name. How can we do this?"

He stepped back. Very slowly he pointed to himself.

"Jim Davis. My name is Jim Davis."

Then he pointed to Danny.

"Fire Eye," Davis said, shaking his head.

Danny understood.

"My name is Danny Blackgoat," he said.

Jim Davis stepped back. His jaw dropped and tears streamed down his face.

"Danny Blackgoat," he said. "My name is Jim Davis. Your name is Danny Blackgoat. I am so proud of you, Danny."

Chapter 11
Fangs of Poison

Mr. Dime never slept soundly. His dreams kept him awake. Sometimes he dreamed of dying in a blaze of gunfire. Other nights he was chased by soldiers and rode his horse off a cliff. But he always woke up, tossing and rolling on his bed, just before he hit the ground.

Tonight's dream was about the rattlesnake. Dime dreamed the snake slithered from the bag and crawled out of the hole. It slid through the gates of the fort and entered the barracks. As if it knew exactly where it was going, the snake came to Mr. Dime's bed.

The six-foot-long rattlesnake climbed up the log wall and hung himself over Dime's head. It opened its mouth and dangled its fangs. Closer and closer it moved to Mr. Dime's face. Finally, it reared back its head, ready to strike.

"NO!" Dime shouted, kicking his legs and rolling to the floor.

When he realized it was just a bad dream, Dime stood up and looked around the barracks. No one heard him holler. But something was strange.

"Where is that Fire Eye boy?" he whispered to himself.

Danny Blackgoat had already left for his visit with Jim Davis. His bed was empty. Mr. Dime smiled.

"I'll have a gift for him when he comes back to bed," he said.

Dime dressed in a hurry and slipped quietly out the door. He crept behind the building and ran to the back gate of the fort. There was no road leading from this gate, only a path winding to the mountains. On most evenings, this gate was left unguarded.

Dime circled the fort and dashed to the campfire grounds. Moving the rock from the hole, he picked up a small tree branch. He tapped the snake through the bag. The rattlesnake jerked and hissed, snapping its jaws and striking. Mr. Dime waited until the snake coiled into a circle, still in the bag.

WHIRRRRR. WHIRRRRR.

He grabbed the snake by the neck and held tight. The snake shook and wriggled, but Dime's grip was strong.

When the snake relaxed, Dime tied a knot at the opening of the bag. Never loosening his grip on the rattlesnake's neck, he ran back to the barracks. He glanced through a window, making certain everyone was still sleeping.

"Good," Dime said. "Fire Eye's bed is still empty."

He entered the barracks and hurried to Danny's bed. He untied the knot. Very carefully he tucked the bag under the covers of Danny's bed. The rattlesnake slithered from the bag and coiled into a circle, waiting.

Ten minutes later, Danny returned from his visit with Jim Davis. Tired and sleepy, he crept across the floor to his bed.

"Jim Davis is like my grandfather," he thought as he crawled into bed. *"He is a wise old man."*

He smiled and whispered the closing words to his grandfather's prayer: *Nothing will change.*

Danny closed his eyes and was almost asleep when change came. He felt something move beneath the covers. Danny waited for a moment.

"What could that be?" he asked himself.

He reached for his ankles. Then he heard it. WHIRRRRR.

Danny threw back the covers in time to see the rattlesnake whip his head back and strike. He sank his fangs deep into Danny's leg, just below the knee.

"Oooooow!" Danny shouted. He grabbed the snake by the neck and yanked it from his calf. A sharp dagger of pain shot up his leg. Danny flung the snake across the room as he fell to the floor.

"Hey! Keep it quiet over there!" a prisoner hollered.

"What's that noise?" said another.

"Hey, Fire Eye's hurt!" shouted another.

Soon twenty prisoners surrounded Danny, who lay on the floor clutching his leg.

"Looks like he's been bit by a rattlesnake. Somebody get the doctor."

"Leave him alone!" a loud voice boomed across the barracks.

The prisoners turned to Mr. Dime.

"He's better off dead," Dime said. "He ain't getting out of this fort alive, anyway. That snake did us all a favor."

The men looked at each other without speaking. Suddenly, without a word, a prisoner dashed out the door. In less than a minute he returned, but without the doctor. Instead, Jim Davis entered the barracks.

"I heard the young man got snakebit," Davis said. "Where is he?"

The men parted their circle and pointed to Danny, rocking back and forth and writhing in pain. Danny looked to his friend, pleading with his eyes.

"Help me, please."

Davis knelt beside him and pulled a hunting knife from his belt. He wiped the blade on his sleeve.

"This will hurt, Danny," he said, "but I have to do it."

Davis took the bottom of Danny's pants leg with both hands and ripped the cloth.

"Looks mighty bad," a prisoner said, and the others took a step back.

Danny's leg was red and swollen, twice its normal size. Danny took one look, closed his eyes, and clenched his teeth.

"Lay back, son," said Davis. "You don't need to watch."

Davis eased the point of the knife into the snakebite. He twisted it deeper, digging out the torn flesh. Danny moaned and his body shook.

"Somebody hold him!" Davis shouted. "Don't just stand there. Give me a hand! You want this boy to die?"

No one moved.

"Oh," said Davis. "I guess some of you do want him dead. Well, that is not happening. Not tonight."

"I'll help," said an older prisoner. "He never did nothing to me."

He knelt down and held Danny by the shoulders. The prisoners looked to Mr. Dime, and in that brief moment, Davis knew who had put the snake in Danny Blackgoat's bed. He also knew now was not the time to deal with Mr. Dime.

With the wound clean, Danny's blood flowed freely, covering the floor in a warm red puddle.

"Clean this up, best you can," Davis said.

The prisoner pulled the sheet from Danny's bed and dropped it to the floor, soaking up the blood.

Davis leaned over Danny and put his mouth on the bleeding snakebite. He sucked the blood out until his mouth was full, then turned and spat on the sheet.

For several minutes Davis sucked the poison from Danny's leg. When the sour taste of the poison was gone, he wiped his mouth and leaned back.

"Tear some strips from the sheet," he said. "Tie the cloth tight around his leg. Just above the snakebite. We have to stop the blood. Don't want him bleeding to death, do we?" he said, glancing over his shoulder at Mr. Dime.

Dime met his look with a mean, cold stare.

"Maybe I'll carry him to my place," Davis said. "I can keep a better eye on him."

Davis rose to his feet and carefully lifted Danny.

"Before I went to war, I had a grandson about this boy's age," Davis said to anybody listening. "I don't know where he is or what's happened to him. But I'm gonna see that nothing happens to this young 'un."

On his way to the carpenter shop, Davis stopped by the officers' barracks. A guard sat in a chair by the door, nodding and snoring.

"You awake?" Davis asked.

The soldier jumped to his feet, knocking his rifle to the ground.

"Yes, sir!" he shouted, looking right and left and trying to remember where he was and what he was doing.

"Can I speak to the officer in charge of the prisoners?" asked Davis.

Soon a young officer stepped to the door.

"This young man, the one you call Fire Eye, was bit by a rattlesnake," Davis said. "With your permission, sir, I'd like to take him to the carpenter shop. The doctor can see him there. He won't be a bother to anybody."

"How did he get bit by a snake in the middle of the night?" the officer asked.

"I don't know about that, sir," said Davis. "He was asleep in his bed when it happened."

"All right," said the officer. "Yes, take him to your shop. I'll send the doctor by in the morning. Will he live till then?"

"Yes, sir. I sucked the poison from the bite. He'll be all right."

"Good," the officer said. "Then carry on."

After Davis left, the prisoners huddled into small groups of close friends. They whispered about what had happened. Everyone knew who put the rattlesnake in Danny Blackgoat's bed. But their fears were not for Fire Eye.

"He'll do the same to us if we make him mad," said one prisoner.

"Somebody ought to do something to him," said another.

"None of us are safe. No telling how many times he's killed before."

Mr. Dime walked from one group to the next, talking loud and slapping the men on their backs.

"Well, that Fire Eye got what's coming to him!" he said to a group standing in a corner.

The men nodded and tried to laugh, but they were too nervous to celebrate.

"Too bad we don't have some whiskey," Dime said. "I feel like partying."

"I'd feel a lot better if we knew where that rattlesnake was," replied a prisoner.

Mr. Dime looked to the floor and said nothing. The barracks grew quiet. Someone had challenged Mr. Dime.

"Maybe I'll find that snake," Dime said. "That's when you'll need to worry."

Ten minutes later a soldier stepped through the door of the barracks.

"All right, everyone back to sleep!" he shouted to the prisoners.

No one wanted to go to bed. The rattlesnake was still in the barracks, maybe hiding under someone else's sheets.

"Move," said the soldier, "unless you want to start your workday now. We can bring lanterns and you'll work twenty hours today instead of ten. It's up to you."

The prisoners shuffled to their beds. They flung back the sheets and lifted their pillows. Some knelt down and looked under their beds.

They found no snake. After biting Danny, the rattlesnake had slithered through a crack in the floor.

Chapter 12
Leather Vest for Jim Davis

The next morning, Davis stood over Danny.

"Son," he said, "I've got some breakfast for you. Easy now, don't move your leg. Just sit up. I'll help you eat." He propped Danny up with a pillow behind his back.

"Thank you," Danny said slowly.

"You are welcome. You are learning, Danny Blackgoat," Davis said with a smile. "Here, I brought you a bowl of oatmeal. Have a taste."

Soon the doctor arrived and looked at the snakebite.

"You saved this boy's life," he said to Davis. "It must have been a huge rattlesnake. I've never seen fang marks this big before."

"That's what I thought," said Davis.

"You are a lucky young man," the doctor said to Danny.

"He can't talk English yet, but I'm teaching him," said Davis.

"Well, keep him in bed and off that leg," said the doctor. "I'll stop by every morning to check on him. Keep the wound clean. If it gets infected, he might lose his leg."

Before every meal, Davis washed the snakebite with soapy water. Danny winced in pain. His leg was red and purple and still swollen twice its normal size. Just as he promised, the doctor appeared every morning.

"It looks fine. Just keep washing the wound, Mr. Davis," the doctor said.

"I'll do that. Thank you," Davis replied.

One morning, after a week of terrible pain, Danny sat up in bed. The sun was peeping through the window.

"Something is different today," he thought.

He felt his leg. The swelling was gone and so was the pain. He looked around the room and spotted Davis stirring his bowl of oatmeal.

"Jim Davis!" Danny said loudly.

Davis was so surprised he dropped the bowl.

"Danny Blackgoat!" said Davis.

He threw his head back laughing.

"Look what you made me do," he said, looking at the puddle of oatmeal at his feet.

Danny laughed too. Davis realized he had never seen his young friend laugh before.

"You are getting well, Danny."

When the doctor arrived, Danny was sitting on the edge of the bed.

"My goodness," the doctor said. "Looks like the poison is gone."

"Yes," said Davis. "He's wide awake today."

"Don't rush things," the doctor warned. "He's not ready to walk on his own, not yet. Maybe let him take a few steps this afternoon, with you holding him up."

After a lunch of beans and bread, Davis sat beside Danny.

"Are you ready to walk?" he asked. He made a walking motion with his fingers. "Walk," he repeated.

"Yes," said Danny. "Walk. Danny walk."

Davis smiled. He stood up, put his hands under the boy's armpits, and lifted him slowly to his feet.

Danny nodded. With Davis behind him, Danny took his first steps since the rattlesnake had bitten him. They walked to the door. Davis took his hands away and Danny leaned against the door, looking outside. The sky was clear blue.

"Just like home in the canyon," he thought.

"Danny," Davis said, pointing to the bed.

Danny turned and slowly walked to the bed.

"I'll be right back," Davis said, and disappeared through the door.

In five minutes he returned.

"I've got a surprise for you, Danny."

Rick and his wife stepped through the door, followed by Jane.

"She doesn't need to see me in bed!" he thought. *"I'm not helpless."*

He flung his legs to the floor and sat up.

"We brought you a gift," Susan said, speaking in Navajo so Danny would understand. She handed Danny a small leather bag, tied with a thin cord. "It's filled with corn pollen," she said.

"*Ahéhé*, thank you," Danny said.

"Your grandfather made it for you," Susan said.

"Do you know my grandfather?" Danny asked. His eyes grew big.

"I know your family," Susan said. "I have been riding to Fort Sumner with Rick. I sought out your family. I wanted to tell them you were safe."

"*Ahéhé*, thank you," Danny said. "How are they?"

"They are well. But Fort Sumner is hard. You know how the soldiers are. You know what they did to you."

"My mother told you?" Danny asked.

"Yes," Susan said. "She told me how every morning she saw you tied to the horse like a saddle. But Danny, she is very happy, now that she knows you are alive."

"When will you see them again?" Danny asked.

"We are going again next week."

"Tell them I will see them again," Danny said. "Tell them I will find a way to come to them."

"I will let them know," she said. "Your grandfather made a gift for Jim Davis too."

She turned to Rick.

"He made this for you," Rick said, handing Davis a leather vest. "I hope it's big enough. I told him you were a big man."

Jim Davis beamed! His face sported a smile as big as the moon.

"He made this for me?" he asked. "Why?"

"Because you saved the life of his grandson, Jim," Rick said.

Davis put on the vest and turned around for everyone to see.

"It's a perfect fit!" he said. "Look at the carvings."

He pointed to an eagle on one side of the vest and a sunrise on the other. Danny nodded.

"Someday I will know the words," he thought. *"Someday I will tell Jim Davis what the carvings mean."*

"Did you tell his family that Danny saved my life too?" Davis asked.

"Yes, I did," Rick said. "Danny, your family is very proud of you."

Though he did not understand all of the words, Danny understood that this was a powerful moment. His family, his Navajo family, had met his new friends.

As if she knew what he was thinking, Jane spoke for the first time. She had been standing beside her mother, listening to all that was said. Sometimes she glanced at Danny, but never long enough for him to see.

"Your mother gave me this," she said, holding up a silver squash blossom necklace.

Danny ran his fingers over the silver flower. He knew this necklace. He also knew his mother wanted him to see this necklace, worn by Jane. The squash blossom necklace belonged to Danny's great-grandmother. It was one of the oldest pieces of jewelry in the family.

"She is telling me something," Danny thought. *"She is giving her approval of Jane."*

"I am glad you met my family, Jane," Danny said.

Jane blushed and turned away. Danny Blackgoat had never said her name before.

Chapter 13
Return to Danger

The next morning, the doctor appeared earlier than usual. He was not alone. A soldier followed him through the door.

"I understand Fire Eye can walk now," the soldier said to Davis. "It's time he got back to work."

"He only started walking yesterday," Davis said. "A snakebite is serious. He needs a few more days to recover."

"That is not for you to decide," said the soldier. "Have him ready to report to work tomorrow morning."

"Yes, sir," said Davis. "He'll be ready. But can I ask a favor?"

"What is it?"

"I think he should stay here instead of the barracks, at least for a while," Davis said. "You and I both know it's not safe for him there."

"That's fine. But he's a prisoner, Jim Davis, same as you. Don't forget it. And don't think you can run things, you understand me?"

"Yes, sir, I do," said Davis. "Thank you."

When the soldier left, Davis tossed Danny's work clothes on his bed.

"Get dressed, Danny," he said. "We're going for a walk."

As they stepped through the door, Davis paused.

"I almost forgot," he said.

As Danny watched, Davis put on his new leather vest, his gift from Danny's grandfather. "I'm wearing this vest everywhere I go."

For the rest of the morning, Jim and Danny circled the cotton fields. Danny understood that soon he would return to work.

From a hill overlooking the cotton rows, Davis halted. He put his arm around Danny's shoulders and pointed to the workers below. There stood Mr. Dime.

"I am afraid for you, Danny," Davis said.

He pulled Danny's pants leg above his knee. He pointed to the scars left by the snakebite and the knife wound. Then he pointed to Mr. Dime.

"He did this to you, Danny."

"Yes," said Danny, pointing to Dime. "He did this."

"You be careful, Danny."

Danny nodded. "Yes," he said.

The next morning, Danny woke up long before sunrise. Davis had water boiling for coffee and oatmeal. After breakfast they walked to the campfire by the cotton fields.

"Take care of him," Davis said to the guards, and turned to go.

Just like before, Danny did everything he could to avoid Mr. Dime. But he soon noticed that something had changed while he was gone.

The other prisoners didn't laugh at Mr. Dime's jokes. They barely spoke to him. No one sat near him at meals.

After lunch, Danny took his hoe and worked a few rows away from the other men. He was chopping a stubborn patch of weeds when heard two prisoners shouting.

"Fire Eye! Fire Eye!"

Danny looked up and saw Mr. Dime sneaking up behind him. He held a jagged rock in his fist. He tossed the rock from one hand to the next. Danny glanced to the guards, but they were too far away to see what was happening.

Dime expected him to run. Instead, Danny stood his ground. He dropped his hoe and looked Mr. Dime in the eyes. He knew that if he fled, if his back was turned, Dime would strike him in the head.

Dime pulled back his arm and flung the rock. It flew past Danny's head, so close he felt the air whistle as it almost nicked his ear. Mr. Dime laughed.

"I'll let you live today, boy. But I won't miss you tomorrow."

He looked to the other prisoners.

"Lucky boy!" he shouted.

Everyone turned away.

"Maybe *you* better look out, Dime," a prisoner shouted.

Now the prisoners laughed. They pointed over Dime's shoulder. When Dime turned to look, Danny Blackgoat stood holding the rock. He was tossing it from one hand to the next. As the prisoners watched, Danny threw the rock across the field, far away from any workers. The prisoners cheered!

Danny Blackgoat made friends that day, friends who would stand by his side when Mr. Dime tried to hurt him. He didn't have long to wait.

An hour after Danny went to bed that night, trouble appeared. Davis and Rick were sitting on the porch of the carpenter shop, talking quietly.

"Sounds like something prowling around the back of the shop," said Rick.

"Something or somebody," said Davis. "We better have a look."

The men rose quietly and circled the shop. They rounded the corner in time to see a man hurry away from the window.

"Did you see who that was?" asked Davis.

"I can't be sure, but it looked like one of the prisoners to me," said Rick.

"I think I know which one," said Davis. "The same man who turned the rattlesnake loose in Danny's bed."

"Mr. Dime?" asked Rick.

"That's who it looked like to me."

Davis struck a match as they approached the window.

"Look," he said, and pointed to several large footprints. "He was crouching at the window. Let's have a look inside and make sure Danny is safe."

Davis lit the lantern as they entered the front door.

"Danny!" Davis called out. "Are you all right?"

"Jim Davis?" Danny said.

"Mr. Dime was outside," Davis said, pointing to the window.

Danny rolled out of bed and flung back the covers.

"Snake?" he asked.

"No, Danny, no snake. Not tonight," Davis replied. "But we're not giving him another chance. Rick, can you stay here tonight and help us keep watch?"

"I'll let my wife know. I'll be back soon," Rick said, and hurried away.

Rick and Davis took turns patrolling the grounds around the carpenter shop. Davis took the final watch. An hour before sunrise he traced the footprints to the prisoners' barracks.

"Mr. Dime will not give up till they bury Danny Blackgoat," Davis said to himself. *"He's not safe here, not anymore."*

Chapter 14
The Gift of Freedom

Every evening, Davis and Danny sat on the front porch of the carpenter shop. One night, after a supper of stew and cornbread, Davis patted Danny on the knee.

"Danny," he said, "it's time we went to work, you and I."

"Work?" Danny asked, standing up as he spoke.

"No!" Davis laughed. "Not work in the fields! You need to learn to talk like I do. Like Rick does."

"Talk," Danny said in a quiet voice. "Danny talk like Jim Davis."

"Yes," said Davis. "I will be your teacher. This porch will be our school."

Danny nodded, and from that moment on his life would never be the same. Davis took his knife from his belt.

"Knife," he said. "Jim Davis's knife."

Danny looked at his friend and smiled. "Jim Davis knife."

"Yes," said Davis. "Say it again. Jim Davis's knife." He handed the knife to Danny.

"Jim Davis's knife," Danny repeated, over and over. He lifted the knife till the blade reflected the moonlight. "Jim Davis's knife."

"Good!" said Davis, pointing to Danny.

"Good," Danny said.

The first night of school, Danny learned to say "rock," "snake," "fire," and "vest."

"Jim Davis's vest," he said proudly, remembering his grandfather's leather shop. He took a deep breath, closed his eyes, and caught the smell of cowhide that filled the air.

"Yes," said Davis. "Jim Davis's vest."

Every night, Danny learned more words. And every morning, he listened to the prisoners speak. He listened when the soldiers gave their orders. He repeated the new words very quietly so no one heard. He practiced talking while he struck the blade of his hoe into the hard ground.

"All right! Get up. Time to work," he said, remembering the words of the soldiers. "I'm sleepy," he said, as Jim Davis said every night when school was over.

By the end of the first week, Jim Davis and Danny Blackgoat had their first conversation. Supper was over and the moon was a tiny sliver in the sky.

"Was supper good?" Davis asked.

"Yes," Danny said. "I like beans."

"Are you sleepy?"

"No, Danny is ready for school."

"Good. First word tonight?"

"Yes, first word."

Davis pointed to the sky.

"Moon," he said.

"Moon," Danny repeated.

"Say it again, Danny."

"Moon. Moon. Moon. Small moon."

"Yes! Danny, you are smart."

"Thank you," Danny said. "You are smart too, Jim Davis."

"I hope so," Davis whispered to himself, recalling the footprints of Mr. Dime outside Danny's window. "I hope I'm smart enough."

He began to hatch his plan. The next evening, as Danny walked from the fields with the other prisoners, a guard took him by the arm.

"Follow me, Fire Eye," he said. He led Danny to the prisoner barracks. "Sleep in your own bed. No more special favors for you."

Soon Jim Davis appeared with Danny's clothes.

"Be very careful, Danny. I've talked to the officer in charge. He said you can still come visit me after work."

"Thank you," Danny said.

"So, I'll see you after supper. School's not out yet!"

That night Davis shivered as they sat down on the porch.

"It is getting cold," he said.

"Yes, cold," Danny said.

Davis carried a book under his arm, the only book he had. He showed Danny the book and said, "I want to read you a story. About a baby. He was born in the cold."

From that night on, as winter approached, school had two lessons. Lesson One was for new words. Lesson Two was for reading.

Every night, Jim Davis read the story about the baby. Though it was only October, Davis wanted Danny to understand about Christmas. He showed Danny the words, touching his fingers to the page and saying them aloud.

"Manger," he said. "Like a barn. Where horses sleep."

Danny understood some words, like *wise men*.

"My grandfather is a wise man," he said.

"Yes, your grandfather is a wise man," Davis agreed, touching his vest.

But Danny had a hard time with the word *angels*.

"They have wings," said Davis, "and they fly. They see everything.

"Eagles," Danny said. "Eagles see everything."

"No, Danny. Angels."

"Like eagles," Danny said. "Angels are like eagles."

"I guess they are," Davis said. He laughed softly and patted Danny on the shoulder. "Maybe angels *are* like eagles."

One night, Davis lit a candle and placed it next to Danny on the porch.

"Candle," he said.

"Candle," Danny said. "This is a candle. Candle."

"Yes, Danny. Candles for the baby. People light candles and remember the baby."

"Candles to remember," Danny said.

"Yes," said Davis. "And they give gifts. Like your grandfather gave me this vest. A gift."

The days and weeks passed, and Danny was learning to speak and even read English. Jim Davis was a good and patient teacher. Susan and Jane visited often. They spoke mostly English, to help Danny learn.

Except for trying to trip him almost every morning, and spitting on him once, Mr. Dime left Danny alone.

One evening in late December, as they wrapped blankets around themselves and began school lessons, Davis waited a long time before speaking.

"Danny," he finally said.

"Yes."

"You know that we celebrate the birth of the baby."

"I know the story," Danny said. "Nobody liked his mother and father. They walked a long walk. Nobody was kind. Nobody let them stay inside from the cold."

"Good, Danny," Davis said. "Go on."

"The baby's mother could not sleep outside. What if a mountain lion attacked? She could never run."

Jim Davis stared at his young friend.

"Son," he said, "you understand this story better than anybody I've ever met."

Davis tilted his hat back on his forehead and looked at the moon.

"I guess the soldiers treated you the same way they treated the baby and his family."

Danny said not a word. The glow of the yellow moon told him that a magic time was coming.

"I have a plan," said Davis. "I want to give you the best Christmas present ever. If you could make anything happen, what would it be?"

Danny smiled. "I would be home with my family," he said. "And my good sheep Crowfoot would be alive."

"Well," said Davis, "I can't do anything about Crowfoot, I'm sorry to say. But I can see that you get home to your family."

"How can you do that?"

"Danny, you have to trust me. You have to do everything exactly as I say. And keep praying with that corn pollen like you do every morning."

"You have seen me pray?" asked Danny.

"Yes, son. I have kept an eye on you. Somebody had to, once you made Mr. Dime angry. I've stopped him from killing you, if you want to know the truth."

"I never knew."

"Well, don't you worry. We're gonna get you out of Fort Davis. Can you find your way home?"

"Yes!" said Danny. "It's a long walk, but I can do it."

Davis laughed and slapped Danny on the knee.

"Son, you won't have to walk! You can ride a pony."

Danny leaned forward and his eyes grew big.

"Here's my plan," said Davis. "You've seen the flags flying at half-mast. Only halfway up the flagpole? Well, they do that whenever somebody dies. It's a way of honoring the dead person."

"I've seen it. We watch the flags every morning from the fields."

"Yes. Well, since I'm the carpenter, whenever anybody dies, I build the coffin. They bring me dried old lumber. Then I nail together a burying coffin."

Danny looked away. To the Navajo people, death was evil and dark. If someone died inside a Navajo house, for whatever reason, no one would ever live in that house again. The family burned the house to the ground and built another. Danny felt very uncomfortable hearing Jim Davis talk about death.

"I don't want to die to see my family," Danny said.

"No, son. You don't have to die. We will wait till somebody else dies. When you see the flags at half-mast, that's the day of your escape. You'll have to act like nothing has happened. Work all day just like you always do. But that night," Davis continued, "after everyone is asleep, crawl out of your bed and slip to the back door of the carpenter shop."

"Will you be here?" Danny asked.

"No, I will stay with Rick and his family that night, so no one will think I had anything to do with this. But I'll leave the door unlocked for you. And here's the important part, Danny. Can you trust me?"

"Yes," said Danny. "You are my best friend. I trust you."

Davis took a deep breath and sighed.

"Danny, I will build the coffin deeper than usual. Room enough for two inside."

"Why room enough for two?" Danny asked.

"Son, I think you know the answer to that. You will open the lid very slowly and crawl on top of the body. Then close the lid and wait."

"I don't like this plan," Danny said.

"Danny, if there was an easy way to escape, there would be no prisoners. They'd all be gone. I know this is scary, but it will work. I know it will."

"What happens next?"

"Just before sunrise, soldiers will come for the coffin. We have to pray they won't look inside. If they do—well, we don't want to think about that. Anyway, they'll have a horse drag the coffin to the cemetery, outside the gates of the fort. The burial service is always at sunrise, so they don't lose any working hours."

"You have to stay in that coffin all day long, Danny. But don't worry. It won't be hot, 'cause you'll be six feet under, as they say. They will bury you alive."

"Jim Davis," Danny said, "I am scared already. I don't like this. My grandfather would never let me do this."

"Danny! Give me chance," Davis said. "Please. What would your grandfather do if someone died in their sleep, on a bed next to somebody else?"

"There is a cleansing ceremony to take the death away," Danny replied.

"Then, Danny Blackgoat, as soon as you are home, tell your grandfather what happened. He will have a cleansing ceremony for you. Trust me, Danny," Davis said, wiping his eyes. "He will be so happy to see you. So will your mother and father."

"Jim?" Danny asked.

"Yes?"

"Why are you crying?"

"Because I will be happy for you, too. But I will miss you. You are like a son to me, Danny."

"We will see each other again, Jim Davis. I know we will."

"I pray that we will, Danny. But you didn't even ask how you're gonna get out of the grave!"

"I think I already know," said Danny. "You'll wait for the sun to go down. You'll slip through the gates of the fort with a horse, saddled and ready for me to ride. You will dig me out of the ground. Is that right?"

"Yes, Danny," Davis said, laughing softly. "You are one smart young man."

"When I'm not in the barracks the next morning, they will look for me," Danny said. "When I don't go to work in the cotton fields, they will think I ran away. But they will never look in the coffin."

"Let's hope not," Davis said. "This is very important, Danny. Let's not see each other till that day. I don't want anyone to see us talking together. Look to the flagpole every morning. When you see the low-flying flag, that will be the day."

"I understand," Danny said. "We don't want anybody to know about our plan."

"That's right, Danny. No more reading and talking lessons. You've learned everything I can teach you, anyway. Let's say good-bye now."

"Good-bye, Jim Davis," Danny said, and stood to go.

"How do you say good-bye in Navajo?" Davis asked.

"Ha-goo-nee," said Danny. "*Hagoonee.*"

"*Hagoonee*, Danny Blackgoat," Davis whispered.

Chapter 15
Mr. Dime's Final Act

What followed was the longest month of Danny Blackgoat's life. Every morning, on his way to the cotton fields, Danny watched the raising of the United States flag over Fort Davis. He heard the bugle sound out the morning song. He watched as the flag climbed the flagpole, all the way to the top.

"On the day the flag hangs halfway high, that is my day of freedom," he thought.

Day after day he watched the flag, only to be disappointed. After a month, Danny decided to talk to Jim Davis that evening.

"I am tired of hoping for something that will never happen. I will stay at this fort till I die. The plan is off," he told himself one morning on his way to work.

Danny heard the bugle call.

"I don't even want to look," he thought, kicking the dirt as he walked.

Suddenly a rabbit sprinted across the path in front of him. Danny laughed. He remembered his grandfather's warning: "Whenever you see a rabbit, Danny, watch your step. Rabbits like to laugh at our expense. Something is about to change!"

With a smile on his face, Danny glanced up. His eye caught the flag, flying at half-mast!

"Yes!" he shouted, pumping his fist and leaping high.

Then he remembered that today must appear like any other day. He recalled the words of Jim Davis: "To anyone watching you, nothing can be different about that day. Eat your meals as usual. Work in the fields as usual. Nothing can be different. Until everyone is asleep. That's when our plan kicks in."

Danny gripped both fists tight and pounded his chest, but in a small and quiet way. His heart pounded with excitement.

"Careful, Danny," he told himself.

Just to be sure, he looked to the flagpole one more time. He tried not to smile, not to celebrate. As before, the flag waved from its freedom perch, halfway up the pole.

Danny sat by the morning campfire with the prisoners, as he always did. He sat as far way from Mr. Dime as possible.

As he finished his coffee and rose to begin work, Danny took his hoe from the guard. Keeping a keen eye on Mr. Dime, he walked to the end of a long cotton row and began hoeing. Every few minutes he looked skyward, making sure the flag was half-mast.

"I have to stop doing that," he thought. *"Nothing can be different about today."*

The first sign of trouble came during lunch. Mr. Dime limped in from the fields.

"I hurt my leg," he said to a guard. "I've never asked for any favors. Can I take the afternoon off? Just let me spend the rest of the day in bed. I'll be ready to go tomorrow morning."

The guards looked at each other. Dime had not been a problem for some time.

"You must spend the day in the prisoner barracks," the officer said. He pointed to a soldier. "You, take Mr. Dime to the barracks and stay with him!"

Following a meal of brown beans, the prisoners returned to their work in the cotton fields. Danny knew that Mr. Dime could never be trusted.

"But if a guard stays in the barracks with him, what trouble can he do?" he asked himself.

An hour later, the guard returned to the fields.

"He left Mr. Dime alone!" Danny thought. *"Mr. Dime is just pretending to sleep."*

Danny attacked his work, hoeing with a fury he had not felt since Jim Davis had his heart attack. The day crawled by. Something was happening back at the fort. He knew it. But he also knew he could do nothing about it.

As the sun neared the top of the mountains,

signaling the end of the workday, Danny's nightmare happened.

POW! POW!

Two shotgun blasts exploded from inside the fort. The guards sprinted to the gates.

"Halt!" shouted the officer. "Don't leave the prisoners!"

The guards returned, but several more gunshots rang out from the fort.

"Stay where you are!" the officer called out. "Gather the prisoners by the campfire. We will wait for orders."

Danny joined the other prisoners, minus Mr. Dime, in their usual places beneath the clump of trees.

"The only enemy Mr. Dime has in the fort is Jim Davis," Danny thought. *"I hope he's safe."*

Danny wanted to dash to the fort, but he knew he would be shot. So, as he had done all day long, he waited. Soon the officer left the campsite and entered the fort.

Darkness settled. A guard built a fire and put a pot of boiling water over the coals.

"If we can't have supper, we can at least have coffee," he said.

Everyone was quiet.

"Too quiet," thought Danny. *"Mr. Dime planned something. I wonder what the prisoners know."*

The officer returned and spoke to the guards in a hushed voice. Danny crept as close as he dared, trying to listen. He heard a few words he understood: "carpenter shop," "killing," "Mr. Dime."

"No!" Danny shouted.

The guards turned to him with wide eyes. They had never heard Fire Eye speak a word of English! Danny hung his head and was silent.

"Don't be so stupid," he warned himself.

His mind was racing. Somebody was killed. In the carpenter shop.

"I know Mr. Dime was there. He went after Jim Davis. That was his plan all along. First kill Jim Davis, then come after me."

He looked up to see a group of soldiers riding to the prisoners on horseback.

"Whatever is happening, it is very serious," thought Danny.

The soldiers surrounded the prisoners. An officer Danny had never seen before stepped from his horse and moved toward the fire, facing the prisoners.

"Stand up!" he shouted. "Now! Make a line and keep a distance between yourself and the next prisoner. You will march in line to the barracks. Anyone who makes a move will be shot. That order comes from the fort commander. You will be under close guard tonight."

"But what do I do tonight?" Danny thought. *"The flag is already at half-mast. We planned my escape for tonight!"*

The line of prisoners marched slowly through the gate and to the barracks.

"When do we eat?" asked a prisoner.

"You will shut up and eat when I say you can," replied the new officer. "Take them to their beds," he shouted to the guards.

The men sat on their beds while six guards, with shotguns handy and ready to fire, stood watching. Two guarded the door.

An hour later Rick and Susan appeared.

"I heard the men had no time to eat," Rick said to the guards by the door. "I brought some dried meat. At least they'll have something in their bellies. After all, this killing's not their fault."

The guards took the bag and reached inside.

"You don't have to look for a knife or gun," Rick said with a smile. "I'm just a delivery man, you all know that. I ain't causing no trouble."

"We have to be careful," said a guard. "We already left a prisoner alone today and look what happened."

Rick rubbed his forehead, covering his eyes. While the guards examined the bag, he searched the room for Danny Blackgoat. When their eyes met, he quietly nodded at Danny, then spoke loud enough for all to hear.

"Tonight is some night, huh? And it's not over yet."

"He is telling me something," thought Danny. *"Something about tonight. If he was warning me, he would not be nodding. Tonight is still on!"*

"Seems safe," said the guard. "All right, men," he shouted. "Stay where you are. We'll bring you supper."

"My wife can make coffee, enough for the guards and prisoners, everybody," Rick said.

"I could use some coffee," the officer replied. "Sounds good to me."

While Susan boiled water over the wood stove, Rick helped the guards pass out the meat. As he approached Danny, he looked over his shoulder. The officer watched him closely.

"Here you are, Fire Eye," Rick said. "And no trouble from you tonight!" Then he rubbed his hand across his lips and whispered, "Escape, Danny. Tonight."

Danny kept his eyes to the floor, nodding to let Rick know he understood.

Soon the coffee was served, but no one spoke. Instead of the usual talking, the prisoners looked at each other without saying a word. Danny knew something was very different about tonight.

"They knew of Mr. Dime's plan," Danny thought. *"But they don't know of mine."*

Soon the prisoners climbed into bed for the night's sleep. A guard put the lanterns out. Darkness and silence settled over the barracks.

Chapter 16
Life Inside the Coffin

Danny rolled over in his bed till his eyes faced the door. He curled into a ball as if he were asleep.

An hour later the officer motioned to the guards, who gathered at the door. As Danny watched, the officer whispered orders. The guards quietly left the barracks, leaving only two guards in chairs on either side of the door.

"They will be there till morning," Danny realized.

Danny's bed was near a window, but he knew the guards would hear the creaking window if he lifted it.

"If I stay alert and wait, the time will come," he thought.

After midnight, a prisoner started shouting. "Help! Help me, somebody! There's a snake in my bed."

Both guards ran to his bedside.

"Don't pay no attention to him," said another prisoner. "He's been having nightmares since the rattlesnake bit that Fire Eye boy. He don't know what he's saying!"

The other prisoners sat up in bed, all wide-awake. The guards took the prisoner by the arms and stood him by the bed.

"Stand here and don't move!" said a guard. He flung back the covers of the prisoner's bed.

"See," said the guard. "No rattlesnake. Now, get back in bed and shut up!"

They prisoners laughed and eased back into their own beds.

"Look at that," said a guard as they passed Danny's bed. "All that noise and he slept right through it."

"Dumb Indian," said the other guard. The two laughed as they returned to their chairs by the door.

But Danny never heard him say it. The prisoner's nightmare was the moment Danny was waiting for. While everyone turned their attention to the hollering prisoner, Danny carefully rolled his pillow and sheet beneath his blanket, so anyone would think he was still curled up in bed. Then he lifted the creaking window, crawled outside, and slowly closed the window behind himself. By the time the guards passed his bed and called him a "dumb Indian," a very smart Danny Blackgoat was standing at the back door of the carpenter shop.

As Jim Davis had promised, the back door to the shop was unlocked. Danny entered and paused at the door. The sky was cloudy and no light flowed through the windows.

In a few minutes, after his eyes adjusted to the darkness, Danny saw the shapes and shadows of the carpenter shop. His eyes settled on the coffin ten feet to his right. He shivered and wrapped his arms around himself.

"There is a body in the coffin," he said in a whisper. "A dead man. Please, Grandfather, stay close to me."

He was more afraid than when the soldiers had burned his home. He was more afraid than when they had shot Mr. Begay. He was more afraid than when they had slaughtered his sheep while he watched. He was more afraid than ever in his life.

Danny cast his eyes around the room. He spotted what looked like another body. It was wrapped in a sheet and lying near the coffin.

"Who is that?" he asked himself. *"No. If Jim Davis was dead, if Mr. Dime had killed him, Rick would have warned me."*

Danny was jerked into the present by voices outside the shop.

"Where could he go?" a soldier shouted.

"No telling," said another. "But if he's left the fort, he'll soon be dead. If the wildcats don't get him, he'll die of thirst."

"Those soldiers are talking about me!" Danny thought.

"Sure is a lot of dying tonight," the soldier said, passing twenty feet from where Danny stood.

Danny walked slowly to the coffin, as if he were taking the last steps of his life. He gripped the lid of the coffin and slowly lifted it. The hinges creaked.

He closed his eyes tight, never looking at the body. With his feet he scooted the legs to one side and stepped into the coffin. He sat on the body and felt a man's stomach sink under his weight. He eased himself back, lying down on the body but still holding the lid over his head. With one final look around the carpenter shop, almost hoping Jim Davis would appear and tell him not to be afraid, Danny Blackgoat slowly closed the lid over himself.

"Now," he whispered, "I wait."

Danny fought sleep, shaking his head back and forth when he felt himself nodding off. Today had been the longest day of his life. Soon he drifted into a deep and dreamless sleep, on top of a dead man.

An hour later he woke up with a shock, banging his head on the lid of the coffin! Two soldiers entered the carpenter shop.

"There's the coffin," a soldier said.

"Careful not to step on that other body," said the second soldier.

"Yeah," replied the first. "Never thought I'd see the day. He was a tough man, but not tougher than a shotgun."

"Where'd he get the shotgun? That's what I want to know."

Danny felt the coffin move as the soldiers dragged it across the floor.

"Man, this is heavy!" said one of the soldiers.

"So is the man inside!" said the other.

Danny's head jerked up and down as they pulled the coffin out the door.

"Go get us a horse," said one of the soldiers. "This thing's too heavy to carry." While he waited for the horse, the soldier sat on the coffin and whistled a song.

"How can he be happy," thought Danny, *"so close to death?"*

When the soldier returned with the horse, he tied a rope around the horse's neck. Then he lifted one end of the coffin while the other soldier looped a rope around it.

"Now," he said, "it's a long way to the graveyard. Let's get started."

The horse dragged the coffin through the gates of the fort and up a steep hill. Danny slid to the rear of the coffin. He stayed completely still and didn't utter a sound. Half an hour later, they came to a halt. The soldiers removed the rope from the coffin.

"I'm ready for breakfast," one shouted.

They walked down the hill, leaving Danny and the body lying beside an open grave. Danny lay still and listened. When he was certain the soldiers were gone, he shuffled till he lay in a more comfortable position.

"Jim Davis said the funerals are always in the morning," he recalled. *"I shouldn't have long to wait."*

At the thought of his friend, Danny remembered the extra body in the carpenter shop.

"Whoever it was, it wasn't Jim Davis," he told himself. *"Rick would have warned me."*

Soon he heard the sound of wagons approaching. A few mourners stepped from the wagons. A soldier, serving as a preacher, carried his large black Bible to the graveside.

The loud voice of the preacher boomed across the mountainside. The funeral was short. No tears were shed.

Soldiers dragged the coffin to the edge of the grave. With little ceremony or respect, they pushed the coffin into the shallow grave. Danny's body slammed against the side of the coffin. He felt a sudden pain as the belt buckle of the dead man stabbed him in the ribs. He wanted to scream, but instead flung his hand over his mouth.

"That's all I need," he thought. *"To come this far, to be so close to escaping, and a pain in the ribs gives me away!"*

Danny felt the sharp edge of the buckle cut through his skin.

"I can't move, not yet," he told himself.

He lay as still as a stone. Something landed on the coffin, catching Danny by surprise. The soldiers were shoveling dirt and tossing it on top of the coffin.

"They are burying the body," he thought, *"and me with it!"*

A cold shiver went through his body. He had not allowed himself to think of this moment.

"If I had known what this would be like, to be buried with a dead man, I would never have done this!"

Dirt and rocks pounded on the coffin lid. Soon the sound was muffled. Then the sound was gone.

The wagons creaked on their way down the mountain, but Danny did not hear them. He was buried in the quiet, dark world of the dead.

As he lay awake in the coffin, Danny remembered his family. He thought of his favorite sheep, of Crowfoot. He smiled, but not for long.

Once more, the memory came alive. He felt two soldiers hold his arms tight. He struggled and called out, but they were too strong. They held his face and made him watch. They called him names he did not understand. And when he grabbed Crowfoot and tried to run, they shot Crowfoot. They shot his favorite sheep as he held him in his arms. They laughed when the blood spurted from Crowfoot. The blood made a puddle on the ground. It flowed like a stream. It flowed in Danny Blackgoat's mind, even today.

"How can they do this? How can they be so mean?"

That is how Danny spent his first hour beneath the ground, buried alive. He remembered the day the soldiers came. He wrapped his arms around his chest and let the tears fly.

Suddenly, Danny heard a voice.

"Danny, you are in the Land of the Dead. You will be cured. Stay strong."

Danny slapped his palms against the roof of the coffin. He flung his arms and elbows against the side of the wooden box.

"No!" he called out.

The voice was that of his grandfather.

"You cannot be dead," Danny whispered. "Please. You are not a ghost, tell me you are not."

The smiling face of his grandfather floated above him. Danny relaxed. His chest heaved and his heart pounded, but he took a deep breath and relaxed.

"It is a vision," he whispered to himself. "My grandfather has come to me in a vision."

He covered his face with his hands and closed his eyes tight.

"How long have I been waiting?" Danny asked out loud.

Less than an hour was the answer, but Danny would never know it. Time crawled by, like memories on the back of a bug creeping across the desert sand.

"I must remember the good things," he told himself.

He thought of his grandmother's thick corn soup. He smiled and his mouth watered, wanting a taste.

"Soon I will taste her soup again. Soon."

He remembered helping his grandfather in his leather shop, cutting the cowhide and making clothes and leather carrying bags. He sniffed the air and smelled the leather.

"You are here, Grandfather," he said. "I smell the leather from your shop."

Danny didn't let himself think of the body below him. His mind flew from one thought to another, always about his Navajo home.

Though he fought to stay awake, Danny nodded off to sleep. When he woke up, he was more scared than ever.

"What time of day is it?" he asked himself. *"No sun, no sky, no moon. How can I ever know?"*

By early afternoon, Danny began to worry about Jim Davis.

"He should be here by now," he thought. *"He should be digging me up. I should be riding a horse on my way home."*

Danny sang Navajo songs, all the songs he knew. By early evening Danny was convinced he had been underground for more than a day.

"Something has happened to Jim Davis," he said aloud. "He was caught stealing a pony. He was stopped by the soldiers. They wouldn't let him leave the fort."

Then the air turned cold.

"He is sick," Danny told himself.

A terrifying thought crossed his mind.

"Maybe he is dead."

Danny remembered the smell of leather whenever he thought of his grandfather.

"Maybe the smell is real."

He took a deep breath. The smell *was* real. Danny Blackgoat smelled the thick aroma of leather inside the coffin.

For the first time, he allowed his mind to think of the body below him. His fingers crept across his chest. Like tiny insects, they crawled across his ribs. Soon his fingers felt the chest of the dead man.

For the first time in his young life, Danny Blackgoat felt the fear of his own death. His fingers felt the vest, the leather vest of his friend Jim Davis.

"Jim Davis will never come to rescue me," Danny said aloud. "He will never dig me out of the ground. He can't. He is dead. My friend Jim Davis is dead and we are buried together!"

Danny took another breath and the smell of leather was stronger than ever. Danny closed his eyes. He whispered the prayer his grandfather had taught him.

When morning casts its light on the canyon walls
A new house is made,
A house made of dawn.
Before me everything is beautiful.
Behind me everything is beautiful.
Above me everything is beautiful.
Below me everything is beautiful.
Around me everything is beautiful.
Within me everything is beautiful.
Nothing will change.

But change came to Danny Blackgoat that day. The air in the coffin grew thinner and thinner.

Chapter 17
Good-bye to Jim Davis

The moon shone yellow and bright, casting long shadows over the graveyard. A few feet above the coffin, a horse whinnied and stomped the ground. An old man picked up a shovel and began to dig.

From inside the coffin, Danny heard a loud scratching sound. A shovel scraped across the wooden lid of the coffin. He held his breath and waited. The lid of the coffin flew open, and there stood his friend Jim Davis!

"Sorry it took me so long, Danny, but I couldn't find a pony," Davis said.

Danny Blackgoat couldn't think of a word to say, but he didn't have to talk. His face reflected the bright yellow moon. He closed his eyes and a grin crept across his face.

"Please tell me you are not a dream, Jim Davis," he said.

"No, Danny. I am not a dream," Davis said. "Oh, how did you like my surprise?"

"What surprise?' asked Danny.

"My leather vest," said Davis. "The one from your grandfather. I put it on Mr. Dime so you wouldn't be afraid."

"You put your vest on Mr. Dime?" Danny asked. He slowly turned and cast his eyes on the body. Mr. Dime lay stretched out in the coffin, looking more peaceful in death than ever during his life.

"I'll tell you what happened someday," Davis said, "but no time for that now."

He stepped back and gripped the reins of a pony.

"It's not as big and strong as I had hoped for. But this young pony is like you, Danny Blackgoat. He's quick and he's smart. You two will get along fine."

"What is his name?" Danny asked.

"Well," said Davis, with a sly grin on his face. "I've been feeding him for about a month now, and I gave him a new name. He's already answering to it. I call your pony Fire Eye! How do you like it?"

"I like it," Danny said. "Thank you, Jim Davis. You are a good friend. *Ahéhé.*"

"We better get you out of here, Danny, before they catch on to us. Here's the plan. Follow the road to Fort Sumner, the one Rick brought you here on. Understand?"

"I understand," Danny said.

"Good," said Davis. "Ride as far from the fort as you can today. I don't know if they'll send any soldiers after you or not. More likely they'll say, 'Let him die,' and be done with it."

Danny hung his head.

"Hey, Danny, that's a *good* thing! They'll leave you alone. Now, about your pony. Fire Eye's already been fed. Ride him fast but let him rest when he's breathing hard. Around noon you should come across a spring of water. Let him drink, but keep a real close eye out. Everybody that takes the road drinks at this spring."

"Why?" Danny asked. He was scrambling for the words. "Fort Sumner, why?"

"Danny, you're not going to Fort Sumner. Listen real close. After the spring, ride for another half day. The hills are thick with cedar trees. Hide in the trees till you see Rick on the road. Make sure nobody is following him."

"Does he know?" Danny asked.

"Yes, he's in on our plan."

"Good," said Danny. His eyes took on a new glow and Davis smiled.

"No, Danny, his wife and daughter will not be with him. But you will see them again, I promise you that."

Danny looked away, embarrassed.

"Rick will lead you to another road, a road going north. After that you'll be on your own. Rick says you should ride to the canyons. Many Navajos are hidden out there, he says, and they'll take you in."

"I understand, Jim Davis."

Davis lifted Danny and placed him on the back of Fire Eye.

"There's food in the saddlebag, Danny. Dried beef, a gift from Rick."

Davis reached for the hand of Danny Blackgoat.

"I'm gonna miss you, son. I don't know what I'll do with nobody to take care of me," he said.

"You took care of *me*, Jim Davis. You kept me alive."

"I guess without each other we'd both be buried in this graveyard," Davis replied. "When all this mess is over with, and you learn to write, send me a letter, Danny."

"I will learn to write, Jim Davis. To make you proud, I will learn to write."

"You best be on your way, son," said Davis. "Take care of your pony and you'll be fine." He slapped Fire Eye on the rump. "Gidd-yappppp!" he shouted.

Fire Eye stomped the ground. Danny held the reins tight and turned his pony north, to Navajo country.

"Good-bye, Jim Davis," he said over his shoulder.

"Good-bye, Danny Blackgoat," said Davis. He watched as Danny leaned forward, urging

Fire Eye into a gallop. He wiped fat tears from his eyes.

"I hope you don't know how much your life is in danger," Davis whispered to himself.

As the sun rose over the desert, Danny pulled Fire Eye to a stop.

"I'll be safe at Canyon de Chelly," he thought. *"But what about my family?"*

He sprinkled corn pollen on the rising sun as he said his morning prayer.

Author's Note: The Long Walk of the Navajos

In 1864, the United States Army, led by Kit Carson, approached peaceful Navajo communities. They burned homes, killed much of the livestock, and destroyed orchards. Over the next few years, they captured almost ten thousand Navajo people and marched them three hundred miles south to Fort Sumner, in Bosque Redondo, New Mexico. There were many reports of cruelty and death during the march, referred to in history as the Long Walk of the Navajos.

The United States Army sought to contain the Navajos on a reservation, opening up Navajo land for American settlers and ranchers. Navajos were determined to live in their homeland, free of outsiders. From the first day Navajos began arriving at Fort Sumner, severe problems occurred. The water supply from the Pecos River was salty and unfit to drink. Many Navajos were placed in tiny adobe rooms with no ceilings and no protection from the freezing weather.

When allowed outside, they had no weapons to defend themselves. Raiders, from Mexico and from other tribes, often attacked the Navajos, kidnapping men, women, and children and selling them into slavery. Navajos also died of disease and starvation.

Following the signing of the Treaty of Bosque Redondo, on June 1, 1868, the Navajos were allowed to return to their homelands. As is common in cases of forced removal, the struggle to survive on the Long Walk remains a powerful component of Navajo thinking. I want to personally share my feelings of deep respect for the Navajo people, the Diné.

Blessings Your Way,
Tim Tingle

About the Author

Tim Tingle is an Oklahoma Choctaw and an award-winning author and storyteller. Every Labor Day, Tingle performs a Choctaw story before Chief Gregory Pyle's State of the Nation address, a gathering that attracts over ninety thousand tribal members and friends.

In June 2011, Tingle spoke at the Library of Congress and presented his first performance at the Kennedy Center, in Washington, DC. He was also a featured author and storyteller at Choctaw Days, a celebration at the Smithsonian's National Museum of the American Indian honoring the Oklahoma Choctaws.

Tingle's great-great grandfather, John Carnes, walked the Trail of Tears in 1835. In 1992, Tim retraced the Trail to Choctaw homelands in Mississippi and began recording stories of tribal elders. His first book, *Walking the Choctaw Road,* was the outcome. His first children's book, *Crossing Bok Chitto*, garnered over twenty state and national awards and was an Editors' Choice in the *New York Times* Book Review.

As an instructor at the University of Oklahoma, Tingle presented summer classes in Santa Fe, New Mexico. Fueled by his own family's survival on the Trail of Tears, he became fascinated with the Navajo Long Walk, and *Danny Blackgoat, Navajo Prisoner* came to life.

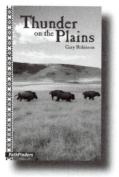

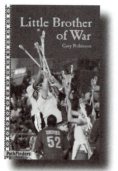